Maggie at Moonrise

Transcendence Book 3

Lynne Cantwell

hearth/myth

Table of Contents

Chapter 1

A month, Rick the lawyer said. It shouldn't take more than a month to wrap up Mom's estate, he said. Her finances were so simple that the worst part would be waiting for the insurance company to pay out on the house.

The house in question had burned down with my mother and my brother Sandy in it. Lucky for me, I survived the fire.

Or unlucky, maybe. I mean, I could see how it looked to the arson investigators: My brother and I had a fight, and so I lit him on fire somehow and ran. The neighbors knew we didn't get along – and hadn't, for pretty much forever. They may not have understood why – Sandy was emotionally and verbally abusive to me ever since we were kids – but they knew there had been stormy scenes recently, when Sandy had left Mom's house in a hurry and in an obviously cranky mood.

What the police couldn't figure out, in the case they were building against me, was why I would have set the fire while Mom was asleep in her bedroom. From outward appearances, Mom and I got along swell. I brought her groceries, ran her errands, took her to the senior center every week. I'd even recently given up my own apartment to move in with her and take care of her as her memory began to fail. But they could have thought I was getting tired of devoting my life to her. There was a fellow in the picture now – Rick the lawyer – and maybe I was ready to move on from all of it, and maybe Rick and I had concocted some crazy plan to kill them both, collect all the insurance money, and hightail it out of town.

I could see how it would look to outsiders. Especially those with suspicious minds.

They were wrong, though. It wasn't at all what happened. But I couldn't tell them what happened, because they would never have believed that a Shawnee thunderbird spirit set fire to my mother's living room in order to move me along faster to the path I needed to walk so I could renew the earth in about ten years, give or take a few months.

That sounded crazy, even to me. And I knew it was true because I'd been there. I'd seen Thunderbird manifest and tell my brother exactly what I thought of his plans to take control of Mom's house so he could pay for the drugs he was hooked on. And afterward I'd talked with Thunderbird, and with the Turtle whose shell we all live on.

It sounds crazy, even now. *I* sound crazy.

As the months dragged by, I began to think I *was* crazy. The arson investigation plodded along, holding up the insurance money, because insurance companies won't pay out if they can find a reason not to, and arson is a slam-dunk of a reason. And I was getting no further communication or instruction from the entities I held responsible for it all. The turtle and bird effigies – ancient copper relics from the Hopewell Indian culture – hung on the chain around my neck, but they were inert. There was no renewal of the antics that had set me on this path: my turtle never rattled, my bird never warmed up or poked me in the breastbone.

And as time went on, I began to wonder whether the popular opinion wasn't right. The investigators couldn't find an accelerant in the charred remains of Mom's house. Rick said that was pretty much the only reason why they hadn't yet charged me with the crime. But he said they knew my cover story, the one I'd told the cops when I was in the hospital, didn't add up, either. I'd claimed that during a short scuffle with my brother, a lamp overturned and the bulb broke, and a spark from the lamp must have caught the carpet on fire. But Rick said the police had discovered the main circuit breaker had been flipped off before the fire started. The broken lamp couldn't have sparked the fire if it had no juice. So they were back to blaming me. They just couldn't figure out how I'd done it.

Maybe I'd gone crazy temporarily. Maybe I had some sort of psychic power that allowed me to call up flames at will, if provoked far enough, like the girl in that Stephen King novel. Maybe, in my altered mental state, I'd made up a story about the turtle and the bird.

Or maybe I'd developed a split personality. I'd had at least one vision – or hallucination, maybe – in which I thought I was the Turtle. I'd thought the Underwater Panther in that vision – or hallucination – was Sandy, but maybe it was me, too. Maybe I was evil. And maybe I was also the avenging Thunderbird. Could I have imagined the bird's attack? The flames dancing on the living room walls? The – something – that protected my back as I was pushed, or stumbled, out the front door as the house went up like a Roman candle?

Rick was almost preternaturally patient with me. "They have no solid physical evidence against you," he said one day, about two months in, as I blubbered in his office.

I sniffed loudly and said, "They could charge me on circumstantial evidence. They do it all the time on TV."

"This isn't TV," he said with a little smile. "Arson always leaves physical evidence. If the investigators can't find it, they have to classify it as a fire of unknown origin. The only thing they have that resembles evidence at all is a statement from a known drug dealer, and that makes anything he says questionable from the get-go."

I knew what he was talking about. Ed Byrum was the neighbor who had called the authorities when the fire started. He had been a buddy of my brother's, and he'd had more than a passing interest in Mom's house; after the fire, he'd blurted to Rick and me that Sandy had promised it to him in payment for the opioids he'd supplied him with.

"But what if they can't find *any* cause?" I said. "I was the last person to come out of the house. And I survived the fire. And I'm my mother's only surviving heir." I fought back a fresh bout of tears. Every time I met Rick these days, it seemed, I dissolved, and it made me disgusted with myself. "It just all looks so *bad*."

"I know."

"How do we make them give up?"

He shrugged. "We wait until they're tired of looking for something that isn't there, or find something more pressing to investigate, and set your case aside."

"How long will that take?"

He shrugged again.

My panic was turning to anger. "You're not helping."

"Sorry, Maggie May. I wish I had something more concrete to give you." He turned to glance at his computer screen for a moment. "You know, we haven't gotten the autopsy reports back yet. Maybe those will be enough to exonerate you."

My eyebrows rose. "Autopsy reports? But it's been months!" The coroner had declared my mother dead of smoke inhalation and Sandy dead of burns.

Rick nodded. "And it often takes months for the full report to come back. Toxicology always takes a while."

"So we wait some more," I said.

He nodded, his gaze sympathetic. After a pause, he said, "How are you doing?"

I raised my hands in surrender. "Oh, just peachy, thanks. Did I tell you my next-door neighbor is a hooker? Sometimes her clients knock her around. That's a lot of fun to listen to."

"Please move in with me," he said. Then he raised his hands. "I'm not proposing anything…"

"I know. We've had this conversation repeatedly." I'd lost everything in the fire except my car and my phone. The Red Cross had found me temporary housing – a room in a rundown hotel on the edge of town, populated with other folks who also had nowhere else to go. Many of the "guests" had clearly given up on finding anywhere else to live, but I hadn't. Rick seemed to think my moving in with him would solve all of my problems – but it wouldn't solve the conundrum of our relationship, or make finding that solution any easier. Which we had also discussed several times. "I want to get out of here, Rick. You know that. I need the insurance payout so I can buy an RV. And the insurance company won't pay if they think they can get away with calling it arson."

"I know. And we'll fight them, if it comes to that." He rose and walked around his desk to pull me into his arms. "It'll all work out, Maggie May," he said into my hair.

"Easy for you to say."

"Come on. I'll buy you lunch."

I pulled away. "I don't think I have time. I need to get to work. I'll have to grab something on the way." I put on my brightest smile and walked to the door. "Keep me posted on those toxicology reports, would you?"

"Of course," he said. He looked bereft.

I walked out anyway.

We had been doing this dance for several months. Rick and I had known each other forever and had run with the same crowd in high school, but I'd lost touch with him after I left college to get married and have my first child. We ran into each other again when Mom needed to have her will redone and the house put in a trust to keep it out of Sandy's hands. While Mom was still alive, Rick had seemed interested in me; then when I responded, he pulled back. Since the fire, he'd been getting pushier and pushier about us getting together, but I was a mess. Besides, I didn't think it would be smart to get involved with my lawyer if I was going to be tried for murder.

I liked him – don't get me wrong. It just didn't seem like the right time.

Although I really did need another place to live. It wasn't just the hooker next door; it was the woman on the other side who sobbed for twenty minutes every night, precisely at 2:00 a.m. I didn't want to know what horror she relived every night. She always looked normal in the morning; we exchanged hellos in the parking lot every day as we got into our cars to go to work.

On the steps outside Rick's office, I pulled in a shaky breath and shoved my hands deep in the pockets of my winter jacket. It was a chilly, raw day, typical for mid-March. I missed my old puffy jacket that had been ruined the night of the fire. This one was fleece, and not as good at keeping out the wind.

I wished fiercely for a strong wind – one that would blow through me, exfoliate me, purify me. One that would blow all of my troubles away.

Instead, it began to drizzle. I hunched my shoulders and hurried to my car. There would be no purification for me today.

I used to be good at waiting. And no wonder – I had a lot of practice. I waited throughout my teen years for Sandy to grow up and move out of the house, so my emotional abuse by his hand would end, and so my mother would no longer defend him. When Sandy finally married, he enlisted his wife to help him continue the abuse – and so I waited until I could go away to college. There, I met another abuser: my ex-husband Gene Brandt. For years, I lived in Rockville, Maryland, with Gene and our children, waiting for him to stop abusing young girls, and waiting for his mother to stop trying to raise our kids herself.

That Ruth had good reason, in her own mind, to try to control my children's upbringing didn't help me. And that my mother had good reason, in her own mind, to try to convince me to get along with my brother – no matter what – also didn't help. Their actions still made me want to get away as soon as possible.

But I had been through a lot in these past six months, and I still had a lot to do. An old woman named Granny, channeling the Shawnee creation spirit Kokumthena, had charged me with renewing the earth, and I knew I had a finite amount of time to get ready to do it – although I still didn't know exactly how to do it. To make things worse, I was aware that the timetable was speeding up, although I didn't really know why.

In other words, I was champing at the bit to get moving on this project.

Unless, as I've said, I was going crazy, and the so-called project was an invention of a diseased mind.

My eldest daughter, Beatrice, is a psychologist. I could have called her; she had helped me straighten out my thinking before. But this seemed like too much to lay on her – and besides, I didn't want her to worry about me. She had her hands full with her husband, their two children, and her job.

I suppose I could have tried to find a counselor close by. But Lawrenceburg, Indiana, is a small town, and options for mental health treatment are limited. I could have driven to Cincinnati, I guess, but then there was the distance, and the issue of taking time off work when I'd already been gone so much. And anyway, I was pretty sure the number of counseling professionals who also have some background in Hopewell deities was zero. I expected I would have better luck finding a shaman or medicine person who had some training in psychology. But I didn't know how to begin the search. I hadn't been looking for Granny and her sidekick Zed; I'd been looking for the Great Circle Earthworks, and they had found *me*.

But something had to give, and fast. My anxiety level was stratospheric. I was snapping at people at work – even at Marty, my favorite bagger. I would bang on the wall and scream when the poor woman next door began her nightly sobbing routine. I had even quit answering my phone every single time Rick called; if he couldn't get me out of this mess, I didn't want to talk to him.

And every night, I would light a candle on the desk in my dreary room and try to contact the spirits that had brought me this far. Somebody. Anybody.

Nobody.

My nadir came in mid-April. I had come home after work feeling dispirited and depleted. I'd brought home a can of soup for my supper, but I forgot that my one decent bowl was dirty from two nights before and I didn't have the energy to wash it in the bathroom sink.

I sat on the edge of the bed and began to cry. How could I have sunken so low? Once, I'd had a three-bedroom house in a lovely suburb, with tasteful furnishings I'd picked out myself. Our master bath had been bigger than this whole tawdry room with the generic landscape in a generic frame hanging above the sagging mattress.

Even in my little apartment here in Lawrenceburg, I'd had lovely things. Not expensive – not as showy as the house in Rockville – but lovely just the same. And now it was gone, all gone. I'd moved it all into my mother's house just a few weeks before the fire that had consumed her life, and Sandy's, and might as well have taken mine.

I took off the necklace that held my turtle and bird effigies and hung it over one side of the straight-backed desk chair. "Why?" I cried. "I don't understand! What did I do to deserve this?"

The effigies, as always, said nothing.

With a roar, I snatched up the necklace and threw it across the room. The bird and turtle landed against the wall near the door – the turtle bowl-side up and rocking, the bird upside-down against the wall.

It didn't make me feel any better. With a sigh, I undressed, slid between the sheets, and flipped out the light.

Sleep took forever to come – but it came with a vengeance.

I was sitting in the guest chair in the living room of my childhood home, but everything looked different. The couch was the wrong color, the windows were in the wrong place, and the kitchen doorway was missing. My mother came down the hall from her bedroom and sat in her chair.

"Mom!" I cried, with a rush of affection. "I'm so glad to see you!"

"Well, I'm not glad to see you," she said tartly. "It's your fault I'm dead."

I froze.

"It's true," Mom went on relentlessly. "If you'd been nicer to your brother, I'd still be alive."

"Mom, he was trying to kill you!" I said. "He wanted both of us dead! He was sick!"

"No," she said, shaking her head. "Not my little boy. Not my Sandy. He hated you, and now I understand why."

"What do you mean?"

"What do you mean?" she mimicked in a singsong tone. "You're the sick one, Margie," she said, using my childhood nickname. "And you don't even know it."

"No!" I said. "I love you, Mom. I did what I thought was best."

"You killed me!" she repeated. "And your brother! And your father, too! You killed your whole family!"

"What? No! How did I kill Dad? I wasn't even here!"

"You just watch your step, missy," she sneered, her hair bursting into flame. "The fire will come for you, too! You'll not escape the flames of Hell!"

I awoke with a start.

I flipped on the light and sat up. I'd had a number of odd dreams and visions, with symbolism and ancient languages that I understood in the dreamscape but not afterward. But this dream was not symbolic in any way. It was Mom yelling at me to get along better with Sandy, as she had always done. And as always, she laid on the guilt.

I recognized all that. But I still couldn't shake the horror.

At that precise moment, the woman in the next room began to sob.

There would be no more sleep for me that night. I got dressed, grabbed my coat, and went down to the car.

I drove aimlessly for a while, and eventually found myself downtown by the casino. The place was open twenty-four hours, and lit up as bright as day. But I didn't go in. I wasn't in the mood for company. Instead, I drove to the far end of the parking lot and got out of the car.

It was freezing. I shoved my hands deep in the pockets of my inadequate coat and walked to the retaining wall. There, I faced the night wind from the river and let the chill seep into my bones.

Only a few cars were out, this late at night. I watched a semi make the approach to the I-275 bridge over the Ohio and disappear into Kentucky. It occurred to me that I could follow that truck to the top of the bridge. There was a narrow walkway along one side of the pavement; I'd seen it from my car window hundreds of times. I wondered what it would be like to swing my legs over the retaining wall and let myself drop. The wind would be fiercely cold; the water, I imagined, shockingly so.

All I had to do was get in my car and follow that truck.

All I had to do…

"Ma'am? Is everything all right?"

I turned, scowling. I hadn't heard the police cruiser ease up behind me, or the opening of the driver's side door. "Yes, I'm fine," I said. "Thank you, officer." And I turned back to my contemplation of the bridge.

But he kept standing there. "Ms. Brandt, is that you?" he said, after a moment.

I turned again, and took a better look at him. Just my luck. "Yes, Officer Pauley, it's me," I said. "How are you?" Pauley was the tall, young fellow who had first interviewed me after the fire.

He walked toward me, smiling tentatively. "I'm fine, ma'am, but I'm concerned about you being out here by yourself. Sometimes folks from the casino get a little rowdy. I wouldn't want you to be in harm's way by accident."

"But it's what I do best," I said.

"Ma'am?" He took another step closer. He was taller than I'd thought. "Are you all right?"

I sighed. "Yes, I am, and thank you for your concern. I guess I should head home now, huh?"

"I think it's best. It's awfully late."

"So it is. I'd lost track of time." With a regretful glance back toward the bridge, I walked toward my car and got in.

Officer Pauley caught the door frame before I could close it. "I'll just follow you home, if that's all right."

"I'm fine, really. You don't need to trouble yourself," I said.

"It's no trouble," he said. "I just want to make sure you get there okay."

For no good reason, tears sprang to my eyes. "Thank you," I said, hoping he didn't hear the catch in my voice. "I think I'd like that."

"I'll be right behind you," he said, and closed the door. And he was as good as his word – all the way to the no-tell motel. He stayed in his cruiser until I had climbed the stairs to my room and waved my thanks. Then he flashed his headlights and drove off.

My room, when I entered, was quiet; the sobbing neighbor must have cried herself to sleep while I was gone. I bent to pick up my necklace, but stopped mid-crouch. It wasn't there.

I glanced around the room, concerned. Had Pauley called for backup? Had someone been in my room while I was gone?

But no, everything appeared to be just as I'd left it. Except for the necklace, which was once again hung over one post of the straight-backed desk chair.

"You knew I'd be back," I said. "You knew I wouldn't jump."

No response. I hadn't really expected one. But I put the necklace on before I went back to bed, and slept soundly for the rest of the night.

Chapter 2

The next evening, as I left the grocery store, I spotted someone next to my car. I slowed my pace and reached into the pocket of my inadequate coat for my keys – the only weapon I had. My concealed fist bristling with keys between my fingers, pointy side out, I approached the car.

"Excuse me," the man called, when I was about ten feet from my car. "Are you Maggie Brandt?"

"Yes." *Who wants to know?*

He clapped his hands together and rubbed them briskly. "Thank the gods. I was about to freeze to death out here." He stuck out a hand. "Name's Dirk Benson."

I would have had to drop my keys to shake hands with him. He seemed harmless enough – not quite six feet tall, brown haired and mustached, and with an engaging smile. But I was wary. I left my fist in my pocket and said, "What do you want from me, Mr. Benson? How do you know my name?"

He whacked his forehead with the heel of his hand. "Of course! I'm an idiot. I should have told you right off. I'm a friend of Zed's."

I let the keys drop back to the bottom of my pocket. "Did he send you? How is he? And how's Granny?" The last time I'd seen them was just after my mother's funeral. Granny had been using a walker – she was recovering from a hip fracture – and she'd told me she was going to have to have surgery for cancer.

"Oh, they're all right. They're in Minneapolis for now."

"Minneapolis! The last I heard, they were in Louisville."

"Yeah, well, that place was driving Granny crazy. Zed broke her out of there and drove her up to the Mayo Clinic. He says it's the best place for her to get treatment for her illness, even though the snow up there is ass-deep until May." He seemed to recollect himself. "Pardon my French."

I waved it away. "So how do you know them?"

"Oh," he said. "I'm a shaman. Say, is there someplace where we could go and chat? Someplace that's not a bar? I'm freezing."

"Steak 'n' Shake or McDonald's. Your choice."

He grimaced. "Steak 'n' Shake it is. I'll follow you." He started for a pickup truck parked two spots over from mine.

"No need to drive," I said. "It's right across the street. See the sign?"

"Oh, right," he said, and laughed. "The cold's addled my brain." He fell into step beside me.

"Where are you from?" I asked.

"Florida."

I laughed. "No wonder you're so cold! How did you meet Zed?"

He looked at me sidelong. "Same way you did, I expect. I more or less ran into Granny at the Bynum Mound and Earthworks in Mississippi."

"What were you doing there?"

"Ritual," he said shortly. Then he relented a bit. "I told you I'm a shaman, right? Well, I've been making the rounds of the Hopewell and Mississippian earthworks throughout the southern states. Granny said she and Zed had been trying to catch up with me for quite a while." We'd reached the restaurant by this time; Dirk held the door open for me.

Inside, I finally got a good look at him. He seemed young – maybe my son Tim's age. "So what sorts of rituals have you been performing at these mounds?" I asked, once the server had settled us at a table and taken our orders.

"Just meditation, mostly," he said, and then paused while the server filled our coffee cups. He doctored his mug with two creamers and a couple of packets of sugar, and then took a long slurp. "Ah, that hits the spot. So what I was trying to do was to reach the spirits of the people buried in the mounds – you know, trying to get a sense of their language, how they'd died, who their descendants were. That sort of thing."

"Why?' I asked. "What would you do with that sort of information?"

He grinned disarmingly. "Worship their gods, maybe." He slurped again at his mug. "I dunno. I felt like I needed to know this stuff, for some reason. Then I met Granny and Zed, and now maybe I have some idea of why I felt that way."

"They're good at instilling a sense of purpose, that's for sure." I sat back as the server brought our orders: a burger and fries for him, a plate of chili mac for me. "You know most of the mounds that still exist have been plundered, right? The bodies and the grave goods are long gone." I dug into my food, trying not to splash chili on my uniform tunic, and remembering my discovery of my own burial mound and the memory of the farmer who had plowed it up so long ago. Well, not *my* mound, obviously; the mound where my ancestor had been buried. And by ancestor, I mean the woman who I was channeling, or something, with the inert pieces of copper hanging on a chain under my tunic. I'd never been clear on whether I was her direct descendant.

"Doesn't matter for my purposes," he said, between bites of french fry. "Psychic impressions can linger long after the body is gone."

I nodded. I'd experienced that, too. "So why are you here tonight? Did Zed send you?"

"Kind of." The conversation lagged while he polished off a chunk of his burger. I couldn't help but smile; my son Tim was the same way around food – single-minded. At last, he sat back. "I was nearby, doing a ritual at Fort Ancient, when out of nowhere I visualized a turtle. It told me that I needed to be here in Lawrenceburg. By that bridge over the Ohio." He tilted his head toward his plate and looked up at me through his lashes. "You know anything about that?"

At the word *turtle* I froze, my forkful of spaghetti and beans dripping over my plate, and looked hard at him. "You don't have to worry about that anymore." The urge to harm myself had passed as soon as Dirk had said the word *shaman*. I realized all I'd been looking for was someone to confirm that the whole thing had been real – that I wasn't crazy. A world that held young men who could utter the word *shaman* as unselfconsciously as Dirk had could also hold a woman who channels a Native American spirit through a copper effigy.

He raised his palms toward me. "All right. Good. I just needed to hear it." He mopped up ketchup with a french fry. "But that's not the only reason I'm here. I also got the impression you have some questions…"

I shouted a laugh so loud that other diners turned to look. "I've got nothing *but* questions," I said, and then lowered my voice. "But the biggest one is when I can get on with my life. The police would like to pin the fire at my mother's house on me, and I can't do anything until that's resolved."

"I have good news for you, then," he said. "It will be resolved within twenty-four hours."

I raised my eyebrows. "Seriously?"

"Seriously." He nodded to reinforce the message. "And you're going to be on your way soon afterward."

I expelled my breath with a *whoosh* and sagged back in my seat. "Well, that's a relief," I said. "I might have to have a milkshake to celebrate." I flagged down our server and ordered a Nutella shake.

"One for me, too," Dirk he told her, and grinned at me. "When in Rome, as they say." Then he sobered. "There's more to the message I have for you, though. Do you want it now, or do you want to have your shake first?"

That sounded dire. The weight that had lifted momentarily from my shoulders was back, but I resolved to be strong. "Let's hear it."

He nodded once, and his eyes took on a faraway cast. "Don't be too hard on your middle child," he said.

"Emily?" I said, surprised. Em had always struck me as the most stable of my three kids. But he went on as if he hadn't heard me.

"The Navajo is to be trusted implicitly," he said. "Go where he would take you, no matter what. Follow the old road to the lake; do not be dissuaded from this part of the journey, as it is crucial. At the pyramids, old wounds will be healed." His eyes focused on me. "Oh, and be sure to stop at Cahokia. Granny left you something there."

My head was whirling. "Should I be writing all this down?"

He grinned as our shakes arrived. "Nah. I mean, you could, but you don't need to. It'll come back to you when it becomes relevant. That's how this stuff works." He plunged his straw into the shake.

I slid my straw into my glass a little more decorously, sipped, savored, and swallowed. "One more question."

"Shoot."

"When I first met Granny, she told me I would shut three doors by myself, and three more would close against me."

He nodded. "Sounds like the sort of thing Kokumthena would say. Go on."

"Okay. So far, by my count, I've shut the three doors on my own, and one slammed shut when my mother's house burned down." I sucked in a breath. "Will the other two... I mean, will it..."

"Will they be as tough as losing your family in a fire?" he finished for me. "Look, Maggie, none of this is going to be easy. I mean, none of it has been so far, right? But I think maybe this one has been the worst for you, personally. The other things you'll be turned away from will be serious, and they will be difficult to take. No question about that. But they won't be as wrenching."

I breathed in slowly and let out the breath the same way. "Okay. Thank you for telling me that."

"Sure thing," he said. "And I hate to eat and run, but I need to get moving." He grabbed the bill and began scooting out of the booth. "I've got this. You stay and finish your shake."

"I can pay for my own supper," I said.

He grinned again. "Tell you what. You can buy me dinner when you get back from your trip." And he left.

I didn't linger long. And as I walked back across the parking lot to my car, I checked my phone to find out the time, and noticed three missed calls, a voice mail, and a text message – all from Rick. I read the text first:

Good news! Call me first thing.

"So it begins," I said, smiling, as I got into my car.

I did Rick's request one better. I beat him to his office the next morning.

"Maggie May!" he crowed when he saw me. "You're a sight for sore eyes. Come on in. Coffee?"

"I brought my own, thanks," I said, raising a paper cup full of the magic elixir. "It hasn't been *that* long since I've seen you, has it?"

He dropped his briefcase on the floor next to his desk and regarded me from the corner of his eye. "Three weeks."

"It has not." I felt my cheeks grow warm.

"It has. I've been marking off the days on my calendar. See?" He pointed to the blotter on his desk. Sure enough, there were little red check marks every day for the past several weeks.

"That's a little OCD, isn't it?"

"Oh, I keep track of lots of stuff this way. Not just you."

"Y'know, most people these days use calendars on their phones for that sort of thing."

"I'm an old fart," he said. "I like to see it all laid out on paper. Have a seat."

I sat expectantly while he bent to rummage in his briefcase. In a moment, he extracted a packet of stapled sheets of paper. He handed them to me with an expectant smile.

The top page was a form with the Indiana state seal at the top. I saw my mother's name – Shirley Denison Muir – and a whole lot of technical jargon. I looked up at him. "I give up. What is this?"

"Toxicology report. Your mom's is on top, and Sandy's is a couple of pages back."

"Okay. Could you translate for me?"

He came around his desk and scooted his other guest chair closer to mine. Then he pointed to something on the first page. "See this?"

"Amitriptyline. Wait – that's Elavil. Mom was on that for years to help her sleep."

"Right. I remember. But the concentration in her stomach was way too high for a single dose."

I looked at him in shock. "Oh, my God. She must have forgotten she'd taken one and took another." I frowned. "But her mind was coming back. We tossed all the over-the-counter meds, and that horrible prescription Diane's doctor got for her…"

"It wasn't just two pills, Maggie." He pointed again to the item. "For that much to show up in the contents of her stomach at time of death, she would have had to take four or five."

I shook my head. "This has to be wrong, Rick. I'm telling you, she wasn't that far gone. You saw her. She was getting better."

"Here." He took the packet from me and found the page where Sandy's report began. "Here we go. Blood test results for your brother." He handed the report back to me.

"Heroin and cocaine?" I looked at him in alarm. "Holy cow."

"And nicotine. Did you happen to smell cigarette smoke when you walked in the house?"

"I don't think so," I said. "But I was focused on other things." Like why the light switch wouldn't work. And like my brother attacking me at the front door.

"Well, here's what I think," Rick said. "I think your brother had some flamethrowers with him."

I cocked my head in confusion.

"Sorry. It's the street name for cigarettes laced with heroin and cocaine. I think he was smoking them either in the house or before he arrived. Then I think he somehow convinced your mother to down those pills."

I gasped. "He could have killed her!"

"Maggie, dear," he said, "he did kill her. The arson team sent an updated report yesterday. They've found the ignition point. It's a spot in Sandy's room." He leaned forward. "I think he dropped a butt in there and it caught something flammable."

"Or he deliberately set fire to my boxes while he was high," I said slowly. "I never did get them up the stairs to the attic. And he'd threatened to get rid of them. He was so mad that I'd moved back in with Mom."

"What was in those boxes?"

I shrugged helplessly. "Everything. Pots and pans, sheets and towels, my summer wardrobe…"

"The fabric could have smoldered for quite a while." He put a hand on mine. "I think you're in the clear, Maggie May."

I drew a ragged breath. "I'm glad, but this is so horrible…" My free hand went automatically to my cheek.

He pulled me to my feet and hugged me. "I know."

My arms went around him and held on. I didn't cry – I felt all cried out – but I needed someone to lean on. That hug from Rick did me so much good.

We stood that way for a few minutes. At last, he pulled away. "I haven't called Columbo yet, but I will do that next," he said. "I wanted to let you know first."

I snorted. *Columbo* was our nickname for Detective Andriotti, the lead officer in charge of the fire investigation. "Can I listen in? I'll be as quiet as a mouse, I promise."

He waggled his eyebrows. "Let's see if he's in." He pulled his desk phone around and dialed the detective's number, then put the call on speaker.

"Do we need popcorn?" I asked as the line rang.

He grinned, but put a finger to his lips.

"Andriotti," the detective said. "Ah, Mr. Hughes. I wondered when you'd call."

"I wanted to tell my client the good news before we talked. She's on the line with us."

"Hello, Detective," I said.

"Ms. Brandt," he said. "I hear you had a little chat with Officer Pauley the other night."

Rick looked at me in surprise. I mouthed, *Tell you later.* Aloud, I said, "I did. Please tell him I'm grateful to him for seeing me home."

"Happy to," the detective said. "Now, as to these reports we received yesterday. Mr. Hughes, I'm sure you have a theory. Let's see if yours and mine match up." I caught a note of humor in his voice.

Rick cleared his throat. "Well, you're the expert, of course. But I think my client's brother arrived at the house before his mother fell asleep, and convinced her somehow to take a number of her prescription sleeping pills."

"She had a prescription for those pills, Ms. Brandt?"

"Yes, she did," I said. "The doctor was weaning her off of them because they were making her forgetful. But she was still taking them."

"And how do you suppose he talked her into taking so many?"

"My brother was emotionally abusive," I said. "He could have bullied her, or he could have confused her to the point where she didn't remember how many she'd taken."

"Gaslighting is the technical term," said Rick.

"Right," said Detective Andriotti. "And the fire, Mr. Hughes?"

Rick glanced at me. "My client tells me she had stored a number of boxes of her personal effects in Mr. Muir's childhood bedroom, in preparation for taking them up to the attic. Quite simply, he didn't want them there."

"I think he set them on fire while he was high," I said.

"Did your technicians find any cigarettes in the fire debris?" Rick asked.

"No," the detective said. "But they found a lighter in his remains, and a pack of hand-rolled smokes in his vehicle. Based on the toxicology results, we're having them tested now." He paused. "We should have done it sooner. It would have sped this process up."

But you were convinced I was guilty. I didn't say it in my outside voice, though.

"How long will those tests take?" Rick asked. "A week, maybe?"

"Less than that, I hope. I've asked the crime lab to put a rush on it. But I have enough to write an interim report that you and your client can submit to the insurance company in the meantime."

I took a deep breath. "Thank you, Detective."

"There's still the matter of the eyewitness who saw someone running through the house in flames," he went on.

"You're speaking about Mr. Byrum," said Rick. "You know, of course, that he's a drug distributor."

"I'm aware of that."

"He was my brother's pusher, Detective," I said. "He told us that right after I got out of the hospital. He said Sandy was going to deed the house over to him to pay off his drug debts."

"Well, well, well," the detective said. "That would have been useful to know sooner."

Rick and I exchanged a guilty look. "I thought I had told you," Rick said.

"I'll check my notes," said the detective. "Oh, Ms. Brandt? There's one other thing."

Yes, Lieutenant Columbo? Aloud, I said, "Shoot."

"I do still wonder why you brought up the broken lamp."

Because I knew you'd never believe me if I said a Shawnee firebird flew through the living room. "Just trying to get the events straight in my own head," I said. "A spark from that lamp seemed likely. I forgot the power was off." I looked at Rick to see if he thought my story was plausible, but his face gave away nothing.

There was a pause. Then the detective said, "Well, that doesn't matter now. We've nailed down the cause of the fire and the perpetrator is dead. We won't be placing charges against you, Ms. Brandt."

Another deep breath. "That's good to hear."

"You may still have a fight with your mother's insurer," he warned. "I have to put arson as the cause on my report, and they may dig in their heels and refuse to pay out. I've seen it happen."

"So have I, Detective," Rick said. "But I have some experience with wrestling with recalcitrant insurance companies, and I'm sure I can bring this one around to our point of view."

Detective Andriotti laughed. "I have no doubt, Mr. Hughes. I'll send over my report shortly." And he hung up.

Rick turned to me with a smile. "Looks like you can start shopping for your RV," he said.

"I might just do that," I said.

His smile faded. "So about your run-in with the law the other night."

"There was no run-in," I said. "I couldn't sleep, so I went for a drive, and ended up in the casino parking lot. I was staring at the river and thinking when Officer Pauley came by on patrol."

"What were you thinking about?" he said, his expression neutral.

I paused, and then thought, *the heck with it. He needs to know what he's dealing with.* "You want to know the truth? I was thinking about how easy it would be to drive to the top of the bridge and jump."

He frowned slightly. "And Pauley convinced you not to?"

"It was more like his presence derailed my train of thought. And I was grateful that he seemed to care." I paused, then blurted, "Rick, I think I've had enough time alone. I don't think it's good for me any more."

"The offer still stands," he said. I knew which offer he meant.

I took an even breath – in, then out. "I'd like to take you up on it."

"Good. Because I think you've been alone long enough, too." His lower lip trembled. "How soon do you think…?"

"I need to ask the office whether I need to give them notice. I'll let you know what they say."

"Sounds good. And Maggie May…" He stopped. "I'm glad."

"So am I," I said.

Chapter 3

The roadblocks cleared rapidly. The report on the contents of my brother's cigarettes came back unbelievably fast, according to Rick. And sure enough, the tobacco was laced with both heroin and cocaine.

We discussed the report over dinner in Rick's dining room. I'd moved my things in the day before, with little fanfare. Rick had offered to help me, but I didn't see the need; I hadn't gained much in the way of stuff past what the Red Cross had given me right after the fire. Two boxes and a brand-new suitcase – everything I owned – made a pathetically small pile in the corner of his guest bedroom. But I told myself it would make it easier to fit my life into a motor home. Other folks have to downsize to do it. I was already there.

"Sandy was an idiot. He could have killed himself," Rick said.

"He did," I said.

"Well, yeah. But what I mean is, at first glance, heroin and coke look like they would counteract each other's bad effects." He paused to chew a bite of chicken and swallow. "Coke is an upper and heroin is a downer. To an addict, it sounds like taking them together would keep him on an even keel. But if he ODs on the heroin, cocaine masks the symptoms. The junkie will sometimes shoot up again, not realizing how close to the edge of death he is."

"You make it sound like he was dead either way." I shivered a little.

He regarded me with a serious expression. "That's pretty much the size of it, yeah."

"Let's talk about something else," I said brightly. "How's the battle royal with the insurance company going?"

"I went another few rounds with them today. But I think I've almost got them convinced to pay the claim. I have to talk to the big guns tomorrow. That should do it."

"Anything I can do to help you?" I asked.

"You could start shopping for your motor home."

"No way," I said. "I want that check in hand first. Too many things have gone sideways for me. I don't want to fall in love with something, only to find out I don't get to have it, after all." I ducked my head and concentrated on the zucchini on my plate. I hadn't meant for the words *fall in love* to slip out – not while we were still figuring out this new twist to our friendship or relationship or whatever it was.

Rick's house, which he'd inherited from his parents, was a split-level, although not as big as the one Gene and I had owned in Maryland. The front door opened onto a wide landing, with the living room down a couple of stairs to the right. A staircase straight ahead led to the two bedrooms upstairs. Rick still slept in the room he'd had as a kid, and used the bigger bedroom at the end of the hall as an office. The guest room was off the living room on the first floor. I remembered when it had been his father's den; now it held a daybed and a computer desk, in addition to a tiny closet. "I know it's small," he said when he first showed it to me. "I could move my stuff into my office and give you my room, if you'd rather."

"Don't be silly. This is fine," I said. "It's bigger than the motor home will be. Plus here, I won't have anyone crying on the other side of the wall at two a.m."

So we had our own territories, more or less, with the kitchen and dining room as neutral ground. It had been different in the old days. As teens, we had often gathered in the living room to watch movies or play Twister; Rick's mom would supply us with pretzels and popcorn, and the kitchen fridge was always full of whatever kinds of pop we were drinking at the time. Later, the Hugheses added a screened porch onto the back of the house, and we would spend summer days there, singing along with somebody's transistor radio and running into the backyard occasionally to douse each other with water from the hose.

"All the times I was over here," I told Rick, "I never thought I'd ever live here."

"I never thought I'd be back after grad school," he said. "So we're even."

After the fire, I hadn't told a lot of people where I was living. I'd shared it with Ron, my manager at the grocery store, because I knew H.R. would need to know. But I hadn't given the address of the no-tell motel to my kids. Part of it was embarrassment and part of it was me trying to save them from worrying. But I also didn't want to have to fend off the inevitable "Move in with us!" invitations. I knew I couldn't leave town while the fire was still under investigation.

Now that things were more settled, though – and especially now that I'd broken free of that horrible motel room – I felt better about giving people my address. So I sent an email to each of my kids – Bea in Baltimore, Emily in Malibu, and Tim in Mexico City – letting them know I was staying with Rick. I also cc'd Riley, who was Gene's second wife, as well as Gene's sisters, Debbie and Abby.

Which, in a roundabout way, explained how Gene turned up on Rick's doorstep a few days later.

It was one of Rick's legal clinic days at the senior center, and I was expecting him home any minute for lunch before he went to his office downtown. I had the day off from work and had promised to have chicken salad sandwiches ready so he could dine and dash. It felt a little 1950s housewifey, but I didn't plan to do it very often. And anyway, I would be leaving soon. He wouldn't have time to get used to me waiting on him.

Anyway, when I heard the knock on the front door, I was ready to give him hell for forgetting his key. And then I opened the door.

"Ah, the little wife," said my ex-husband sarcastically. "Mind if I come in?"

It only took a moment for me to figure out what had happened: Riley had told Ruth where I was, and Ruth had told her son. Gene and Rick knew one another from our college days, and had never been buddies. And I'd heard through the family grapevine that Gene was in an in-patient pedophilia treatment program at a facility near Cincinnati – just a hop, skip, and jump from Lawrenceburg. If I'd thought it through sooner, I would have realized a visit from him was inevitable. Especially once he heard I was living with Rick.

"Actually, yeah, I do mind," I said. "What do you want, Gene?"

He raised his hands in an expansive gesture. "I was in the neighborhood, that's all. I thought I'd stop by and see how you were doing." He dropped his hands. "I heard you had a rough time a little while ago. Sorry about your mom."

"Thanks," I said shortly. "I'm doing fine. How's your treatment progressing?"

He ducked his head and looked around. "Do we have to have this conversation out here? Can I at least come in and have a glass of water or something?"

I curled my lip in disgust.

"Maggie," he said, cajoling me. "It was a long drive, and I need to piss."

I rolled my eyes and opened the door. "Bathroom's back that way," I said, pointing down the hall. "Next time, don't buy the Super Big Gulp."

He laughed. "Remember that time you…"

"Bathroom's that way," I said, stone-faced. I did remember the time, but I knew what he was up to: he was trying to get me to lower my defenses. If he got me to laugh, then I'd be halfway to his side. And I didn't know yet why he was here.

"Okay, okay," he said, hands up in surrender and laughing at his memory of me, eight months pregnant with Beatrice, rushing out of the car to a gas station bathroom, fifty miles after I'd first told him I needed to pee.

I'm sure it had been hilarious from his perspective.

I went back to prepping the sandwiches for Rick and me. I heard the toilet flush and the bathroom door open. The next thing I knew, Gene was right behind me, his hands on my waist. "Mmm," he said. "I haven't had your chicken salad in a long time."

"Well, you're not getting any today, either." I slid away from him to fetch two plates from the cabinet above the sink, but I didn't have time to grab them before he was on me again.

"Maggie," he said, nuzzling my neck. His hands roamed up my torso toward my breasts.

I squirmed away again and faced him. "Look, Gene, apparently I didn't make myself abundantly clear months ago. So here it is again: Whatever you're selling, I'm not interested."

He took a step toward me. "You won't give me another chance? You don't have anybody now – your mother's gone, your brother's gone. Your father's been gone for ages." He took another step. "All you have is me."

I couldn't help it – I laughed uproariously. "You sound like my mother," I said when I could draw breath. "'Be nice to your brother, Maggie. When I'm gone, he'll be all you have left.' Right. I wonder how she feels about him now that he killed her and tried to kill me, too."

Gene's eyes grew wide.

I pressed my advantage. "It's taken me decades, but finally, *finally*, I can smell a scumbag coming – and I know better than to get involved with one, ever again." I planted my fists on my hips. "Get out."

He rushed me and mashed his mouth against mine. My lower teeth cut into my lip, and I tasted blood. "Get...OFF...of...me!" I yelled. I pinwheeled my forearms up to break his grip. Then I pushed him – not hard, but enough to send him across the kitchen, arms cartwheeling.

"What the hell is this?" Rick said from the doorway to the dining room.

"Well, hello, Rick. I was just getting a little something from my wife," said Gene, smirking as he righted himself.

"*Ex*-wife, " I reminded him hotly.

"Looked to me like she was giving as good as she was getting," said Rick. "Get out of my house."

Gene, furious, raised a fist toward Rick. "Eugene Brandt!" I yelled. "If you hit him, I'll call your parole officer!"

He froze.

"Do you want to go back to prison?" I said. "I'm sure it's lovely there."

"Don't drop the soap," Rick said with a cockeyed grin.

Gene roared and lunged at him.

"Oh, for God's sake," I said, as the two men, both pushing sixty, grappled in the middle of the kitchen. I reached in and shoved them apart. "Gene, if you don't leave now, I will call the police. I mean it."

"Ow. Jesus, Maggie." He rubbed his breastbone where I'd just pushed him away. Rick had landed a punch somehow in the melee, and I could see a spot on Gene's cheek beginning to swell as he glowered at him. "This isn't the end of it, Hughes," he said. "I'll be back."

"No, you won't," I said. Rick just pointed silently.

Gene glared at each of us in turn as he stomped toward the front door. We followed him to make sure he actually left. He opened the door and looked between us. "She's a lousy lay anyway," he said to Rick, and slammed the door behind him. Rick went to the door and threw the deadbolt. A few seconds later, I heard a car start and drive away.

I got as far as the dining room before I sagged into a chair. "Are you okay?" Rick asked. "Your mouth is bleeding."

I put the back of my hand to my sore lip. "Cut my lip on my teeth when he kissed me."

Without a word, he got a wet washcloth and handed it to me. I winced as I pressed it against my bottom lip.

"How did he get in?" Rick asked, pulling up another chair.

Ruefully, I said, "I let him in. He said he had to pee. I should have told him to try the gas station up the block."

"Did he do anything…?"

"No," I said, looking directly at Rick. "Just the kiss. But I'm glad you came in when you did."

"So am I." He looked out the window for a moment, as if to reassure himself Gene was really gone. Then he looked back at me. "I've been thinking about this cross-country trip you want to take."

My eyes grew wide. "Don't tell me not to go," I said. "I'm going, whether you come along or not."

"That's what I'm…" He glanced away again. "I think I need to come."

I dropped the wet washcloth on the table. "To protect me?" I said. "Really, Rick?" I probed my lip. "Ow."

"I'll get you some ice," he said, springing up and heading for the kitchen. "It's gonna swell up."

"Not as bad as Gene's eye will," I said. "Nice shot, by the way. That year you spent on the boxing team in high school finally paid off."

"Thanks." He dropped some ice cubes in a ziplock bag and brought them to me. "Wrap the washcloth around it."

"I know how this works, Rick. I raised a son. Although Tim didn't get into many fights." I winced again as I put the washcloth to my lip, but the ice felt good.

"I'd like to meet him," Rick said. "And Emily, too."

"Well, come along, then."

Our eyes met over the improvised ice pack. "I think I will," he said.

Chapter 4

A few days later, the insurance company finally surrendered and agreed to pay off the claim on my mother's house. Finally, my way was clear.

Rick and I celebrated at Whisky's. He ordered a steak; I settled for seafood linguine, as my lip was still a little sore, and hoped I didn't splash any Alfredo sauce on my blouse.

"Time to buy that RV, huh?" he said as he sawed at his steak.

"Don't rush me," I said. "I'd like to savor the size of my bank account for a minute."

He grinned, chewed, and swallowed. "*Now* is it time?"

I laughed and whacked him on the arm. "I think you're more excited than I am."

"You know what they say about boys and their toys," he said. "Do you know what kind you want?"

I swirled my fork in my linguine. "I definitely don't want a humongous motor home," I said. "Too hard to maneuver and too hard to park."

He nodded thoughtfully. "What about a trailer? Then you could drop it at a campground and go."

"True. But I was thinking more along the lines of a Class C." It seemed like a good compromise to me. I'd still be driving a bus, essentially, but there would be enough room for two people without us constantly tripping over one another.

"That's a decent size. Have you ever been in one?"

"No. Have you?"

"I looked at them right after my divorce. I toyed with the idea of chucking it all and living like a nomad for a while."

"What stopped you?"

"Mom got sick." He dove back into his steak.

I felt like a jerk. "That's right. I'm sorry."

He waved it off. "It's fine. I've had a lot of time to get over it." He looked up from his plate. "But the idea never went away."

I smiled. "So once you've been bitten by the wanderlust bug, you're never cured?"

"Something like that." He cut another bite of steak. "Have you planned out the route yet?"

"Other than seeing Emily and Tim? Not really."

"You know, Maggie May, we're going to have plenty of time. Neither one of us has a job or a family to rush back to. We could do this up right. See a bunch of places we've always wanted to see." His eyes sparkled.

"I suppose you have a list," I said drily.

"How did you ever guess?"

It was a long list. It started with Sault Ste. Marie, Michigan, and went across the Upper Peninsula to Duluth, Minnesota. From there, he wanted to tick off a few places in South Dakota – Mount Rushmore and the Black Hills – and then to Wyoming for Devil's Tower ("I've wanted to see it in person ever since *Close Encounters of the Third Kind* came out"), the Tetons, and Old Faithful. Then Seattle, and then a drive down the coast, all the way to San Francisco.

"What? No sequoias?" I teased him.

"We could stop there, sure, if you want to. But I want to ride a cable car." And from there, the bright lights of Los Angeles; San Diego, because the weather was rumored to be perfect; and across the Mojave Desert to the Grand Canyon.

"You skipped Las Vegas," I said, pointing to the map we were poring over.

"Did I?" he said. "Too bad, huh?"

I laughed. "No, I'm okay with that."

"Good. Glad that's settled." And on went his list: Arches, Mesa Verde, Carlsbad Caverns. Dodge City in Kansas. Oklahoma City and the memorial to the victims of the bombing there. The Alamo. New Orleans.

Then up the Mississippi to Memphis. "Barbecue and the blues, Maggie May! Although I could take or leave Graceland," he confided.

By this point, my head was spinning – and we had barely touched the eastern half of the country. "Have you ever been to any of these places?" I asked, thinking maybe there were a few we could skip.

"A few," he said, "but you haven't been to *any* of them. And if you don't go now, when will you do it?"

He was right, as far as that went. "But I have my own list," I said, and ticked them off: Malibu, to see Emily; Cahokia Mounds in southern Illinois, because Dirk said Granny had left something for me there; and wherever else my muse – or the urging of my effigies – took me. And Mexico City, to visit Tim.

He regarded me for a moment with that *I swear I'm not judging you* look that he must have perfected through years of listening to accused criminals' hard-luck stories. "Are you sure you want to drive a motor home to Mexico City?"

"Why not?" I said. "They have roads in Mexico, don't they?"

"They do, but that's not the point." He paused. "There's a lot of criminal activity down there. Drug lords and gang killings and so on. A motor home sporting Indiana plates would stick out like a gringo in a Mexican bar."

"You think I'd be a target." It wasn't a question.

"I think we'd be better off parking the bus in El Paso or Albuquerque and flying down to see Tim."

"Let me think about it," I said. We talked a little bit more about the trip, but the fun had gone out of the discussion for me. The point of buying the motor home was to make the trip. The trip included seeing Tim and meeting Ana. It was beginning to feel like *my* trip was being overwhelmed by Rick's plans for *our* trip – which looked a lot like the plans he'd made for *his* trip.

I'd been married for a long time; I understood how relationships worked. I knew that if I let Rick come along, I'd have to compromise. It just felt like he was already asking me to give up too much.

I managed to put him off the RV shopping trip for a few days, but at last, he wore me down. We picked a day and set out, bright and early, for the closest RV mega-superstore, which happened to be north of Cincinnati.

"Can we go to Serpent Mound, too?" I asked as we got on the road.

Rick, who had insisted on driving, glanced over at me. "Why?"

"Because I'd like to see it. I've never been there." And Shaman Dirk's mention of the place had piqued my interest.

"But it may take a while at the RV place to see all the models. Maybe we could do Serpent Mound another day."

I gave him a dubious look. "Right. Which other day? We're leaving in a week for the West Coast."

"Well," he said reasonably, "we could stop in on our way back."

Or we could stop today, after I've had my fill of looking at motor homes. But I didn't say it aloud. I just let him keep driving.

The RV dealership seemed to have hundreds of Class C motor homes. Our salesman, whose name was Bob, asked a few questions – "Where you folks headed? What features did you have in mind?" – and then led us up and down the aisles, showing us a bewildering array of buses and boxes-with-trucks-attached. I *oohed* and *ahhed* over the first ten or twelve, and then they started to run together in my head.

And too, some of the price tags were out of this world. "This one is worth more than Mom's house," I whispered to Rick as we climbed up into one unit. It had a full-size shower, a washer-dryer, two slide-outs ("It's super roomy," Bob said), and a fireplace, together with the price tag displayed prominently on the passenger side window.

"What do you have in used units?" Rick asked. "Anything comparable to this?"

Bob paused in the act of lifting up the dinette cushions to show how the table dropped down to make a bed. "Well, now," he said. "We do have a real nice unit that just came in on a trade-in. It's last year's model, comparably equipped to this one. It's gonna be priced at about thirty grand less than this one, I'd say, but I could knock off another twenty grand for you folks."

That was still more than the insurance check. By a lot. "Let's take a look at it," Rick said. "Okay, Maggie May?"

"Great!" Bob said, and led the way to the used units.

It was a long walk. I used it as an opportunity to try to talk some sense into Rick. "That's still more money than I have," I said quietly.

"Let's just look," Rick said. "This is like car shopping. I can haggle the price down to something more in your ballpark."

"It's going to have to be a hundred grand less to be in my ballpark," I said. "You know how big the check was."

"Well, let's look at it anyway," he said. "If we can't get the kind of deal you need, I can help you pay for it."

I stopped. "I don't want you to help me pay for it. I want an RV I can afford."

"Lovers' quarrel?" Bob called from a few yards ahead of us.

I gave Rick a disgusted look. "We're just friends," I told Bob as we resumed our trek.

Rick's eyes lit up as soon as he saw the trade-in — and just as fast, I knew it was not for me. It was easily thirty feet long, with a slide-out, a queen-size master bedroom, and truly hideous red-and-black buffalo-check fabric covering everything from the sofa to the dinette cushions to the curtains.

"What, no fireplace?" I said to Rick out of one side of my mouth.

"Maybe we can get them to throw one in," he said quietly. Louder, he said, "Tell me again how much this would go for, Bob."

"Well, I'm not sure we've priced it yet," he said, eyeing me. Clearly, he'd pegged me as the stumbling block in this deal. "Let me go talk with my manager while you folks poke around a little more in here." With a friendly wave, he left us inside the unit.

"It's too big," I said immediately. "I wouldn't feel comfortable driving it. It would be like driving a semi."

"I can drive," Rick said.

"I know you can drive. That's not the point."

"But this is such a great unit!" he said. "Look – there's a skylight!"

"I hate the upholstery."

"And all these storage cabinets!" He swung an arm wide, as if he were the eye candy on a game show, showing off the prize behind Door Number Two.

"Rick," I said. "Everything I own fits into two boxes."

"And a suitcase," he reminded me, opening what proved to be a closet. "Which would fit great right here."

I crossed my arms. "You're not listening to me. I don't want to buy this RV."

He closed the closet door. "I know. It's too big. Let's ask him if we can see something else."

Forty-five minutes later, we still hadn't seen anything I liked. It was getting toward lunchtime by then; I was getting hungry, and Bob was beginning to look annoyed that he'd spent his whole morning with a couple of browsers.

Rick took the hint. "Look, I'm really sorry we wasted your time today."

Bob waved us off, his salesguy smile back in place. "No problem. I get it. It's like shopping for a house. No sense in buying the first thing you see, right? Better to wait for the one that's perfect." He leaned over to Rick. "My wife's the same way."

I was this close to reminding him that we weren't married, but Rick shot me a warning look as he laughed and agreed.

"Just go on home and sleep on it, and I'll call you in a couple of days," Bob said. "Fair?"

"Absolutely," Rick said. Hands were shaken all around, and we commenced the long, long hike back to Rick's car.

I felt better after we ate. There was a Mexican place across the street from the dealership, and we laughed over our burritos at some of the worst things we'd seen that morning.

But as we headed to the car, I felt a familiar tug on my sense of direction. "How far is Serpent Mound from here?" I asked Rick as we got in.

"I have no idea. Why?" He looked at me. "You want to go *now*?"

"Why not? We've got all afternoon."

"Well, but…" He started the car and began backing out of the parking space. "We've blown the whole morning and we haven't bought an RV yet. And we were planning to get on the road next week."

"*We* haven't bought an RV yet?" I said in surprise. "Stop the car."

"What?"

"I mean it. Pull back in."

With his exasperation barely concealed, he shifted into drive and parked again. A car that had been waiting for our space gunned his motor and sped past us. "You're making us friends all over," he muttered, glancing at the rear-view mirror. Then he turned to me. "Okay. What?"

"Whose trip is this?"

"It's ours."

"No," I said. "It's *mine*. And you need to understand that I will be spending part of it working."

He didn't quite crack a smile, but it was close. "Working? For whom?"

I pulled my necklace out from under my shirt. "See these guys?" I said. "They're in charge. They've been in charge ever since I first set foot inside the Great Circle Earthworks last fall. Now, we can pick an itinerary. That's fine. But there are going to be days when these two are going to hijack the schedule."

"I see," he said. "And right now, they're hijacking your purchase of a motor home?"

"Right now," I said evenly, "they want me to go to Serpent Mound. And they will make my life difficult if I don't go right now today."

To be honest, I wasn't sure that was true. I'd always just bowed to the impulses the effigies caused me to experience; I'd never actively fought against one. But it was as good an excuse as any. And if Rick was going to come along with me, he needed to understand whose desires came first.

He looked at me for a few moments – waiting for me to grin, maybe, or at least to tell him I was joking. When I didn't, he sighed and plucked his phone from its mount on the dashboard. "Okay," he said, bringing up a GPS app. "I guess we're going to Serpent Mound today."

I stifled an impulse to thank him. Instead, I nodded silently and looked out the window.

It took us a little over an hour to get to the park. We drove past newly-planted fields and stands of trees sporting the bright green leaves of spring. Here and there, dogwood trees showed their pink and white flowers.

As we neared the park, I glanced over at him. "Archaeology was never your thing, was it?"

"I prefer people to be alive and able to respond to questions," he said, with a touch of asperity. Then he glanced at me and relented a bit. "But I know it's always been your thing."

"I would have made a career out of it if I hadn't gotten pregnant," I said. I'd long since stopped kicking myself for that mistake. It had given me Beatrice, and then Emily and Tim, and I wouldn't trade them for anything. Still, I wished I'd been able to do both – have children and a career. Which I could have done if I'd married just about anybody but Gene.

"Did your wife work?" I asked Rick as he made the turn into the entrance to the park.

"Yeah," he said. "She was a lawyer, too." He glanced over and must have seen my look of surprise. "I never told you that?"

"Nope. Never."

"Huh. I guess it never came up." He navigated around the parking lot and pulled into a vacant spot. He sucked in a breath. "Yeah, we met in law school. That happens a lot, actually. You're all together in this pressure-cooker environment, all taking the same courses. You get to know one another pretty well." He shoved the gearshift into park and killed the engine. "Or you think you do."

"What kind of law did she do?"

"Family law. Miserable business."

"Worse than defending criminals?" I asked, aiming for humor.

He raised an eyebrow in my direction. Then he settled back. "If you want to meet people when they're at their best, don't take up law," he said. "But with criminal law, you're trying to help someone put their life back together – assuming you get them off. In a divorce, though, you're always tearing people's lives apart. Always."

"Sometimes, divorce is a good thing, though," I said quietly.

He let my comment hang in the air, unanswered. Then he got out of the car.

As we walked up the path toward the earthwork, he changed the subject. "What are we looking for here?"

"I don't know," I said honestly. After the original tug I'd felt in Cincinnati, my internal homing instinct had gone quiet. "Let's just walk around for a little bit."

"There's a visitor center," he said, and we made our way toward it.

I picked up a brochure as Rick made small talk with the staff member behind the cash register. The earthwork, it said, was 1,348 feet long – overshooting the Hopewell Indians' magic number of 1,054.

"Who built it?" I heard Rick ask the cashier.

"Good question," she said. "We used to think it was the Fort Ancient culture, sometime around 1,000 A.D. But archaeological digs are still happening here, and radiocarbon dating now points to a much earlier date for the serpent's construction – around 300 B.C."

Rick turned to me as I joined them. "That's earlier than your Hopewell folks, isn't it?"

"Yeah, but they knew it was here," I said with sudden certainty. "And they took care of it for many years."

The cashier eyed me with some suspicion, although not as much as I might have expected. Then I remembered the Serpent had attracted a fair amount of attention from New Agers over the past few decades. I was likely not the only person who'd ever showed up here claiming to know something about the site's ancient history – although I might be one of the few who actually did. She turned to Rick. "That may be true. We've seen evidence that the Fort Ancient people rebuilt sections of the earthen berm where it had eroded naturally."

I nodded and wandered away again, toward the reference books. I picked up one at random, then froze as a familiar voice spoke in my ear. *Hopewell, Adena, Fort Ancient. Convenient labels for the alien culture who could not believe your people were capable of building such monuments.*

I wheeled with dread, hoping I wouldn't see flames licking at the walls. To my relief, there were none.

Rick and the cashier looked up at me in surprise. "Do you want to get that?" Rick asked, indicating the book I still held.

I glanced down. *An Archaeology of the Sacred* was the title. "Sure," I said, and pulled out my wallet.

As we left, the bag tucked under my arm, Rick asked, "What happened back there?"

"I thought I heard something," I said vaguely. "The serpent's this way."

We passed an unmown meadow. I could see the coils of the serpent to our left. "There's the tail," Rick said, noting the direction I was looking in. "Want to climb the tower?"

"Why not?" So we made the long climb to the top of the observation tower. The view did not disappoint; from there, we could see the whole serpent, from its spiral tail to the egg in its mouth.

All at once, I knew whose egg it was. "It's not a serpent," I said. "It's a water panther. And it's eating Thunderbird's egg."

Rick studied me. "Looks like a snake to me," he said.

I shook my head. "It's an early depiction of the myth," I said. "It changed over time. But that's the story this earthwork is telling." I placed my hands on the railing and leaned forward. "A number of Native American tribes have myths in which Thunderbird is at odds with a water monster," I said, drawing on some of the material I'd studied in college, forty years before. "The Woodland Indians believed water was the way to the underworld, and a Water Serpent, or an Underwater Panther, was a sort of guardian of the way. The Sioux have a similar myth about the creation of the Badlands: Thunderbird fought and killed a giant water serpent called the Unktehi, and in the process, all the water in the river boiled away."

"How did the Sioux end up with a Woodland Indian myth?" Rick asked, leaning one elbow on the railing.

"They started out as a Woodland tribe," I said. "Their enemies forced them to relocate to the Plains. Let's get closer."

"You said the serpent here is eating Thunderbird's egg," he said.

"Right. The Serpent is trying to defeat Thunderbird by keeping her from hatching. I think." I shook my head. "These aren't my people, you understand. But that's the sense I'm getting. Which means that's the way the Hopewell interpreted the story."

"Let me see your book," Rick said as we reached the ground again. I handed him the bag, and he pulled out the book and began flipping through it. "It says here the serpent's coils are aligned with the constellation Scorpio, as it crosses the heavens during the course of the year," he said. He looked up at me. "And the oval aligns with the sunset on the summer solstice. The author believes it's a sun symbol."

"Yeah, well, he's wrong," I said. "It's an egg. Come on."

As we walked along the path, the centuries dropped away. I had trodden this path before, but closer to the coils – not on top of the berm, but close. Very close. The old path began at the tip of the tail and went around and around, in and out, alongside each of the coils, and then back again on the other side. It was meditative – like walking a labyrinth.

It was the height of summer – nearly sunset. My shaman lay curled inside the oval, awaiting his rebirth. We had arrived by canoe to a landing spot on Brush Creek, just below the promontory where the Great Serpent did its mischief. We had climbed up to the top of the cliff, and now we sang and chanted, weaving our way to the Serpent's mouth and the mortal danger it represented. With our voices and our drums, we were Thunderbird, and we must chase away the Serpent and rescue our egg, so that the seasons would continue to turn.

We reached the Serpent's mouth, and there I, Thunderbird, made my stand. I climbed up the berm to the Serpent's head, and planted my talon-spear straight through his eye. The drums beat a wild tattoo as we danced, mimicking the Serpent's death throes.

At last, the dance ended. I leapt down lightly and ran to my egg. Now our followers began to sing again – a new song, encouraging my egg to hatch. I circled the egg, encouraging new life to spring forth. Slowly, my shaman began to uncurl. At last, he stood and shook himself. Then with a few quick taps, he broke the shell and stepped out, into my arms. Our people sang of triumph as we sank to the ground and…

"Maggie May?" Rick said. "Come on back."

I shook my head, dazed, and looked around. I'd taken a seat just at the edge of the egg's berm. I looked at Rick, shocked. "I didn't climb that thing, did I?"

"No, but it looked like you wanted to." He held out a hand and pulled me to my feet. "You're flushed."

I put the back of my hand to my cheek. "You would be, too, if you'd been on the verge of making love in front of your tribe," I said with a laugh. "What happened?"

"You got a weird look in your eyes, and started chanting," he said. "Then you crossed over to the earthwork." He pointed. "I was surprised nobody stopped you, to tell the truth. But anyway, you were walking alongside the coils. When you got to the head, you put one foot up on the earthwork and shouted something. Then you went to the oval and kind of collapsed."

"That's pretty much what I did in my vision," I said, "except with a bunch of people chanting with me. And drumming." I could almost hear the drums, still, beating in time with my heart.

"So who was the guy who…?"

"My shaman," I said. "He was curled up in the egg. We sang to him to help him break free of the egg. Then the old Thunderbird and new one would mate at sunset. The idea was to remake the world and all that." I realized, belatedly, that Rick was still holding my hand. "And then the old Thunderbird would die."

His eyes widened. "You were sacrificed?"

"No, of course not. No more than the shaman was actually born and no more than the Water Serpent was actually killed."

"But you actually had sex."

"I think so." I raised my shoulders and grinned. "We'd pretty much have to, if it was a fertility rite."

We started back along the path toward Rick's car. "How did you get chosen to be the Thunderbird?"

"I never told you? I was a shaman, too."

He pulled me to a halt and stared at me.

"Why else would I have these?" I said, pulling out my necklace. The bird, I noticed, was warm – warmer than it would have been from simply laying against my bare skin – and emitted a soft, golden glow that pulsed in time with my heart, in time with the drums I still heard faintly in my head. Rick touched it, and I shivered. Then the light went out.

His mouth dropped open, and he drew back both of his hands.

"Well," I said brightly. "I think we're done here. Let's go find the car."

Chapter 5

Rick was subdued on the way home, although maybe he was just thinking – wondering what he was getting himself into, maybe, by taking a cross-country trip with a middle-aged woman who believed she was the reincarnation of a Hopewell shaman.

I didn't have much energy to spare for his ruminations. My own mind was going a mile a minute, committing details to memory. As before, both in the Great Circle and at my own burial mound, I had perfectly understood the ancient language spoken while I was immersed in the vision or memory, but could not recall a single word of it now. What I remembered were the feelings, and the intent behind the words I had chanted and sung.

And to a degree, I remembered what had come afterward. For I knew that during that very public mating, my shaman and I had conceived a child. And while I didn't recall exactly what had become of that child, the emotions attached to his memory were achingly sad.

In this mood, with a foot seemingly in each world, I felt a strong pull toward a farmhouse up ahead. "Rick," I said, breaking perhaps a half-hour of silence. "We need to stop up here."

"Where?" he said. "Why?"

"I don't know why, but we do. That house right over there."

We were in the middle of nowhere, with fields on one side of the road, the corn just coming up, and a small subdivision on the other side. The farmhouse was on our right and visible across the expanse of empty fields.

"Okay," Rick said with a sigh of resignation.

Five minutes later, we pulled into the driveway. Parked by the road, just off the drive, was a Class C motor home with a homemade FOR SALE sign, made with a beat-up piece of corrugated cardboard and a Sharpie, stuck under one windshield wiper.

A man our age, dressed in overalls, came out of the barn to meet us. "Can I help you folks?" he asked as we got out of the car.

"How much are you asking for the motor home?" I asked. I already knew I was going to buy it; my turtle had begun banging around on my chest as soon as I stepped out of the car.

"Thirty thousand," the man said. "Want to see it?"

"You bet I do," I said.

"All right, then. Let me go in and get the key." And the man went up the steps to the screened porch and disappeared inside.

Rick turned to me. "That's a steal."

"I know." The units we'd been looking at that morning had been five or six times that much.

"Don't get your hopes up, Maggie May," he said. "It might be a dump inside."

But it wasn't. It was perfect. It had a cab-over bed, a tiny but adequate bathroom, and even a little electric fireplace.

"The fireplace is adorable," I said.

The man beamed. "My son, Dan, put it in. I thought he was crazy, but you'd be surprised how many times we used it." He looked around. "Yep, we had some good times in here. Dan and me used to take it up north to go deer hunting, just about every year."

"And he doesn't want it any more?" I asked.

The man's eyes clouded over. "He got killed in Afghanistan."

My heart lurched. "I'm sorry," I said. And I was – because now I remembered what had happened to my own son so long ago: he, too, had been killed in battle. Our lucky son, the fruit of the world's rebirth, had died as our world was ending.

"It's all right," the man said automatically. "Anyway, the wife isn't interested in camping. She always says, why should she pack up and go someplace in an RV? She'd just have to do all the chores she does at home, only with less space."

Rick and I laughed politely.

"Anyway, well, I just don't have the heart to go hunting without Dan. So I figured I might as well sell this thing. But those thieves over at that big dealership in Cincinnati wanted to give me pennies for it," he said with a frown. "'It's too old,' they said. 'If you think you can get a better price, sell it yourself,' they said. So I am." He cut a glance at each of us. "Business has been pretty slow, though. To be honest, you folks are the first people who have stopped to look."

"Well, you only need one buyer, right?" I said cheerfully. "And I'm definitely interested."

Rick nodded. "Can I take a look under the hood?" he asked.

"Why, sure," the delighted farmer said, and the two of them scooted past me to the door.

While Rick pretended to know something about cars — oh, come on, he's a lawyer, not a mechanic — I sat at the dinette and surveyed my new home. Then I pulled out my turtle and bird and set them on the table before me. "This is it, isn't it?" I asked. "This is our chariot."

In response, Turtle did a little dance on the tabletop.

I tucked them away again and pulled my checkbook out of my purse. Half an hour later, my bank account balance was $30,000 lighter, but I was behind the wheel of my very own RV, with the title tucked away in my purse.

Back at Rick's place, we jockeyed vehicles in his driveway so that the motor home was parked closest to the house, with my car behind it. I had no intention of driving the RV back and forth to work. Not only would the mileage be terrible, but I needed to go to the Bureau of Motor Vehicles to finish up the paperwork.

Rick slapped the side of the RV as I got out. "Well, here it is, our home away from home," he said. "Ready to hit the road?"

"Not right this very minute," I said with a laugh. "First, our home-away-from-home needs Indiana plates. Second, we need to finish mapping out our route. And third, it's suppertime and I'm starving."

"So am I," he said, leading the way into the house. As soon as I got inside, he shut the door behind me and took me into his arms. "To be perfectly honest," he said in my ear, "ever since you mentioned that fertility rite, I've been hungry for something else."

"Oh, really?" I said.

"Mmm." He kissed my temple, my cheek, my lips.

I slid my arms around his neck and pressed myself against him. "You sure you want to do this?" I said, my voice low.

"It's purely a practical matter," he said, his hands caressing my back. "This way we'll only have to make one bed in the RV."

"I've always liked that about you," I sighed as he planted tiny kisses along my jawline.

"What's that?"

I licked his ear. "You're so practical."

Supper was very late that night.

I had the following day off from work, as well. We lounged in bed for a few hours, and then I showered and got dressed to visit the Bureau of Motor Vehicles.

While I stood in one of their interminable lines, Bea called. "Hello, honey," I said. "What's new?"

"Wow, Mom," she said. "I've never heard you so happy. Where are you?"

"In line at the Bureau of Motor Vehicles," I said.

"That's even weirder. Nobody likes going to the DMV."

"I'm just in a good mood, that's all," I said. "I bought an RV yesterday. I'm really gonna do this thing, Bea. I'm really going to drive across the country to see Emmy."

"That's great!" she said. "I'm so glad you're getting on with your life, after all the craziness over the past six months."

"I am, too," I declared. "So what's new with you? How's John? How are my beautiful grandchildren?"

"John's fine. Royce and Ryker are fine – growing like weeds, of course," she said with a laugh. "But that's not why I called."

"Oh?"

"Have you heard from Dad?"

I hadn't told her about Gene showing up at the house to seduce me. "Not lately," I fudged. "Why?"

"He's going to prison."

My eyes widened. "Prison? You mean jail, don't you?"

"No, I mean prison." She went on to explain that Gene had checked himself out of the treatment facility a couple of weeks back, and had been arrested while lurking outside a high school in Milan, Indiana. The school called the cops when a group of female students came to them to complain that a man was trying to pick them up. He told the arresting officers that he only wanted to see the high school featured in the movie "Hoosiers." When they ran his driver's license, they discovered he was on a national index of pedophiles – and in fact was violating parole.

"I looked up Milan online," Bea said. "That's pretty close to Lawrenceburg."

"Just up the road, yeah," I said, putting concern into my voice. "When was this?"

She told me. It was the day after he'd been at Rick's house, pestering me.

"To be honest," I said, moving up with the line, "he did stop by to see me. Rick came home from work for lunch and found him in the house, and we kicked him out."

I heard her sharp intake of breath. "Are you okay?"

"We're both okay. And I'm not surprised to hear that your father's in trouble again. Sad, but not surprised." I shook my head. "I'm sorry, Bea."

She sighed. "You know, Mom, it's funny. I keep thinking I'm over being surprised at the things he does, and then he does something even stupider."

I laughed in sympathy. "I know what you mean. Does Em know? And Tim?"

"I'm going to call them next. I wanted to check on you first."

"That's very sweet, honey." I smiled. "Wait. How did you find out about this?"

"Riley told me. She's still listed as his next-of-kin."

Of course she was; they were still married, as far as I knew. "That poor girl," I said. "I'll have to give her a call. Uh – what about Nana? Does she know?"

She sighed again. "That's why Riley called me. Nana basically collapsed when she told her. She's been in bed ever since."

Ruth was given to dramatics. But this seemed extreme, even for her. "What does John think?" Bea's husband was Ruth's internist. Ruth once claimed she'd introduced them, but I'd never asked Bea whether that was true.

"He wouldn't tell me. Doctor-patient privilege, or so he claimed. But he looked worried, Mom."

"And now you're worried, too."

"Well, yeah," she said. "I just lost one grandmother. I'm not crazy about losing the other one. Even if she is a pain in the butt."

"I hear you," I said. "Well, I can't come out there right now…"

"No one's asking you to," Bea said sharply. "Riley and John and I are handling it. We don't need for you to come and fix it. We're all grownups, you know."

I straightened, worried now myself. "I never meant to imply you weren't." Bea hadn't spoken to me for years after the divorce. We had just recently managed to patch things up – and here I was, saying stupid stuff that might make her angry enough to stop speaking to me again. And I couldn't bear that. I couldn't lose her again. "I'm sorry."

"I'm sorry, too," she said after a moment. "We're just all kind of on edge, that's all."

"I'm sure it's stressful," I said sympathetically. "Everything's stressful when Nana is involved. But you guys will be fine."

"Thanks, Mom," she said, sounding mollified.

I almost said, *and if you need advice...* But I managed to stop myself. I'd just crawled out of one self-dug hole; the last thing I wanted to do was dig myself another one. Instead, I said, "Keep me posted on her, okay? And your dad, too."

"Sure," she said. "Enjoy your trip. Tell Rick we said hi."

"Love to everyone there," I said. "Give the kids extra hugs from me." I ended the call and stowed the phone in my pocket. Some of the light was gone from my day. I didn't like to think about my kids having to deal with adult problems – but of course, they had to. We all do.

The hardest part of parenting, I reflected, is letting them grow up.

Chapter 6

On a sunny morning in mid-May, Rick locked up his house and we hit the road.

After the tussle we'd had over RV shopping, I expected a fight over the route for our Grand Tour. But I was pleasantly surprised. Rick happily agreed to postpone the northern part of his original route – which would have taken us up to Minnesota, South Dakota, and eventually the Pacific Northwest – in favor of a more direct route to Los Angeles through St. Louis and Oklahoma City. "We'll still be able to see a lot of the things I wanted to show you," he said, as we mapped out the final route in bed. "I mean, the things I wanted to see."

"Uh-huh." I dropped the map to the floor and scooted closer. "So you did have an ulterior motive for coming along."

He ran the backs of his fingers along my bare arm. "Nothing ulterior about it," he said. "I was going to be right up front about my motives." He bent his head to kiss my shoulder. "Eventually."

I was half convinced he was being so agreeable because we'd brought the maps into the bedroom with us. But I knew that wasn't really it. He'd been more amenable ever since my vision at Serpent Mound, and I suspected that seeing the magic in action had made somewhat of a believer out of him.

That hadn't been the first time he'd seen my effigies do tricks – they'd put on a little show for him on our first more-or-less-official date – but this was the first time he'd seen any sort of result. Before, he could have written it off as sleight of hand. But this – being urged to drive to the park, hearing me say things with a certainty I could not possibly possess from what I could have learned in this lifetime, falling into a fit of sorts, and then leading us unerringly to the RV we were now riding in – this was not so easily explained away.

So when I told him we needed to make Cahokia our first stop, he agreed without question.

Morbid curiosity, maybe.

He did extract a promise from me, though: For every detour that the effigies and the spirits of the land dragged us out on, he would get to pick a destination nearby that was on his list. "Fair's fair," he said. "One for you and one for me." And he'd already picked out his first post-detour site: the Gateway Arch in St. Louis.

"No problem," I said. "We're going to drive past it anyway."

"Oh, no," he said. "That's not good enough. We need to get out of the car and actually tour the thing."

I shrugged. "Fine with me. The view should be spectacular."

So that was the plan as we left Lawrenceburg and crossed the Ohio over the I-275 bridge – the same one that I'd contemplated stepping off of, just a few weeks before. As we reached the top of the span, I cut a look at Rick. He regarded me with a serious expression.

"What?" I said, although I knew where his mind had gone. After all, mine had gone there, too.

"If you ever have an urge like that again," he said, "tell me. Deal?"

"Yes, all right," I said with a sigh. "But I don't expect things will ever get that bad again."

"You didn't think they would be that bad the first time."

I nodded, keeping my eyes on the road. "True enough."

We passed the *Welcome to Kentucky* sign. "Unbridled Spirit," I quoted.

"That's the last we'll see of the Hoosier State for a while," Rick said. "You don't ever have to come back, though, do you?"

I'd been thinking about that. I'd been living at Rick's house long enough that I'd begun to settle in. And especially after I began spending every night in his bed, it had started to feel like home – as much as any place had felt like home since I'd left my kids behind in Rockville. "I don't know," I said with a small smile. "I liked it okay at your place."

Then I jumped. Because out of nowhere, a door went *slam!* in my head.

"You okay?" Rick asked.

"Fine," I said, but I was shaken. I wasn't sure of the parameters – whether the restriction encompassed all of Indiana or only Lawrenceburg – but I was certain of one thing: I would never move back into Rick's parents' house again.

We were within spitting distance of the park before noon. I was too impatient by then for anything as mundane as making lunch, so we grabbed something at a fast food place. I don't even remember which one. That's how antsy I was about this stop.

What had Shaman Dirk meant when he said Granny had left me something here? What was it? How big was it? How would I find it? And would I be able to get it out to the RV without the guards stopping us? Because if it were any sort of artifact, taking it would very likely be a crime.

Rick looked nervous, too. "You won't fall into another fit in there, will you?"

I shrugged. "Honestly, I have no idea. It's not like I get a warning ahead of time. It just happens."

He pointed to my chest, where my effigies nestled in their usual spot under my shirt. "What do your buddies there say?"

I pulled them out and looked at them. "What do you say, guys?"

Nothing. Of course.

"You're no help," I groused as I slipped the necklace back inside my shirt.

Rick laughed, which made me laugh, too. But I don't think either of us felt any more relaxed.

I was too nerve-wracked to drive from the restaurant to the park, so I handed the key to Rick. He got us parked, and remembered hats and sunscreen for us both. The temperature wasn't supposed to be blistering, but we would be walking around what amounted to an open field with little shade to speak of.

Archaeology peels back layers to get a tantalizing glimpse of the past
– and often, especially in America, it happens on a deadline. I'd read up a
little bit on Cahokia while waiting for the insurance company to pay out
on Mom's house, and I knew that many of the discoveries about the
ancient city had been made as developers waited – with backhoes and
cement trucks, metaphorically if not literally – to move in and pave
everything over. The site's importance wasn't really understood until the
federal government decided to build Interstates 55 and 70 smack-dab
through the middle of Cahokia, thereby freeing up federal funding set aside
by the legislation that created the interstate highway system. Once the
archaeologists had some idea of what they were dealing with, the interstates
were re-routed north of the major portion of the ancient city. It was
declared a UNESCO World Heritage Site in 1982.

I'm not using the term *city* lightly. Cahokia in its heyday – around 1050
A.D. – had a population bigger than that of Paris at the time. The
archaeological record indicates the city went through three successive
building periods: the first, in which homes were built around centralized
courtyards; the second, in which the ceremonial center of the city was built,
and homes were built on a grid, similar to cities planned today; and the
third, in which the ceremonial center was apparently abandoned and
people went back to building their homes around central courtyards again.
After about 1300 A.D., everybody seemed to have vanished. By the time
Europeans found the place, it was a ghost town. Nobody knows why,
although there's been plenty of speculation, ranging from flood to famine
to marauding bands that caused the central elite to erect a stockade around
their part of the city.

All of which is to say that the Cahokia site is *big* – bigger than any
other archeological site I'd been to so far. The highway that leads to the
park entrance bisects the ceremonial center of the city. I nearly got
whiplash from looking at the ruins on either side of the road.

We parked the RV and headed for the interpretative center, intending
to grab a map and brochure or two and get out to walk the grounds. But

not far from the door, an exhibit caught my eye. "I'll meet you," I said vaguely to Rick, and allowed myself to be drawn to the display case as if by some magnetic force.

One of the artifacts on display was a red flint-clay figurine of a woman with a determined look on her face. Her legs straddled an odd-looking creature, and she was attacking it with a hoe. I glanced at the explanation next to it, and caught my breath. The creature the woman was attacking was described as a massive serpent with the head of a bobcat and a branching tail.

"It's a Water Panther," I said.

"The Birger figurine?" someone at my elbow said. I turned to see a woman, maybe in her forties. "It's a fascinating piece, isn't it? They say the red goddess is trying to cultivate the Underwater Panther. See how its tail is growing up her back and producing squash?"

"Yes, I see that," I said.

"Some of these so-called experts think the Underwater Panther is a fertility figure."

I stepped back, stunned. *A fertility figure? Are they crazy?* "It's not."

"I know," she said. "You must be Maggie."

"I am," I said. "And you are…?"

"Janie. Janie McClatchey." She offered her hand, and I shook it.

"Did Granny send you?" I asked.

She laughed. "How did you ever guess?"

I tapped the side of my head with a forefinger, which made her laugh harder. "No, but honestly," I said, "I'm just starting to get the hang of this. I met a guy named Dirk in Lawrenceburg, Indiana. He told me I needed to be sure to stop at Cahokia, because Granny had left something for me here. Are you the thing she left for me?"

"Oh, goodness, no," she said, her hand to her chest. "I can't go anywhere with you – I work here. But I have the thing she left for you. Come on." And she led me toward the center's help desk, where Rick was chatting with one of the staffers.

"Hi, Stan," Janie said to the staffer with a wave. "I need to get something out of my locker. I'll be right back. Don't move," she said to me, and disappeared down a hallway.

"Not a chance," I called after her.

"Making new friends?" Rick said as he slipped an arm around my shoulders.

"She knows Granny," I said.

"Ah." He nodded. "Well, *my* new friend, Stan, tells me there are active digs all over the place here."

"Mr. Hughes says you're interested in archaeology," Stan said. He was younger than my own kids, and exuded enthusiasm. "Maybe you'd like to sign on to help at one of our digs. Some of the local universities have programs you could get involved in."

"Thanks for the suggestion. I'll check it out," I said politely. "But I'm really more interested in the Hopewell culture. Cahokia is Mississippian, right?"

"Oh, sure," he said. "But we've found some Hopewell artifacts here. Let me show you." He led us to an exhibit that featured artifacts in a wide range of styles, including a human torso cut from mica that I immediately pegged as Hopewell.

"These were all found here?" I asked, bending to inspect the items. "That's extraordinary."

"Cahokian society was quite cosmopolitan," Stan said. "They appreciated beautiful objects, just as we do today. Think of the way we revere the Dutch masters, say, or Michelangelo's David. Well, the Cahokians were the same way."

Rick had moved on to a nearby case. "Was there trade between the Cahokians and the tribes in Mexico?" he asked Stan. "I'm no expert, but these look Pre-Columbian to me."

"Oh, no," Stan said. "Those are from Cahokia."

"Really?" said Rick.

I walked over to take a look myself. "But that's Mayan imagery," I said. "Mayan or Toltec."

"Nope," said Stan. "The iconography is similar, but it's Mississippian."

"It's *very* similar," I said, and looked again at one piece. There was something about it that made me shudder.

"You okay?" Rick asked.

"Fine. It's extraordinary, though, just like you said." I looked again and suppressed another shiver. "I'd swear it was Mayan. Or even Aztec."

"There you are!" Janie called from the exhibit entrance.

"Oh, sorry," Stan said, hunching his shoulders and smiling ruefully. "I kind of got carried away. I forgot they were waiting for you."

"It's okay," Janie said with a smile. "You weren't that hard to find. But there's a crowd at the help desk."

"Oh! Right. Sorry again. Nice talking to you folks." And he scurried out.

Janie watched him go. "That boy is brainless sometimes," she said, shaking her head. "Here." She handed me a folded slip of paper.

I unfolded it. An unfamiliar name and phone number were written on it in a precise, Palmer-method cursive. "Someone you know?" I asked her.

"Someone Granny knows. She said you'll need to contact him when you get to the Four Corners area. Were you planning on going there?"

Rick and I traded a look. "I guess we are now," he said.

"So how did you meet Granny?" I asked her.

"Same way you did, I suppose," she said. "The first time I met her, my life was a lot different. I'd just escaped a bad relationship in St. Louis and was driving to Chicago to try to find a new job and rebuild my life. For some reason, I decided to stop here."

"The car made the turn by itself," I said.

"Yes!" she said. "Exactly."

"Same thing happened to me at the Newark Earthworks," I said to Rick.

"Anyway," Janie resumed, "I had sort of a religious experience or something over there, near Monks Mound." She waved in what I assumed was the direction of the pyramid. "Granny happened by and helped me put my experience in perspective."

"She never just 'happens by,'" I said.

"I figured that out later," said Janie. "Anyway, I never made it to Chicago. I got a job here and stayed." She smiled. "And every now and then, Granny and Zed stop by for a visit. Or to drop off something for someone else, like you. Oh!" She clapped her hands. "Here I'm going on and on about me, and you've come to see Cahokia. Don't let me keep you any longer. Did Stan give you a map?"

"Got it right here," Rick said, brandishing a brochure.

"Good. Well! Enjoy!" Janie gave me a hug and left by the same doorway Stan had.

"Well!" Rick said with a lopsided grin. "Shall we go forth and enjoy?"

I rolled my eyes. "Sure. It's what we're here for."

The site, as I've said, is big – too big to absorb in one visit. We wended our way amongst mounds and earthworks, past borrow pits filled with water, and around a recreation of part of the stockade the elite had built toward the end of Cahokia's heyday.

"I wonder where Janie had her fainting fit," Rick mused as we approached Monks Mound.

I barely heard him. Suddenly there was a roaring in my ears. Once again, the present-day dropped away, and I was transported to the past – but this time I was only an observer. And glad of it. Because what I was witnessing was an attack on a pre-stockade Cahokia by another tribe from the south.

Don't ask me how I recognized the attackers' battle dress as Aztec, but I was certain that's who they were. The Cahokians had knives and their famous hoes, but they weren't skilled in battle the way the Aztecs were. Plus the Aztecs were better equipped. In short order, they had overrun the temple that was now called Monks Mound, and were carting off many spoils of war: beautifully wrought copper goods, shells, and commoners. Slaves.

I came back to the present, shivering and leaning on the recreated stockade for support. "Maggie May?" Rick asked, concerned. "I thought these weren't your people."

"They aren't. Weren't. But my people had some experience with the attacking forces."

His brow furrowed. "I don't get it. I thought the Hopewell…"

"Not the Hopewell. The Shawnee." I pushed myself upright and started walking again, with Rick by my side. "We can go up to the top of the pyramid, can't we?"

"You mean Monks Mound, right?" He consulted the map. "Yeah. There's a viewing platform up there. But are you sure…?"

"I think I need to," I said. I held out my hand, and he laced his fingers tightly with mine. I gave him a grateful smile.

His, in return, was grim. "I have to tell you that it makes me a little crazy to watch you have these spells when I can't do anything to help."

"You *are* helping," I said. "Just being here is helping, believe me. I've had visions at times when I had to get back to the car on my own afterward. It's not a lot of fun."

"I just hope I don't have to carry you," he muttered.

We reached Monks Mound after a short walk, and began climbing up the 154 steps to the top. No further visions assailed me, for which, I could tell, Rick was grateful. We were both sweating and breathing hard by the time we got to the top, but it was mainly because the humidity had begun popping up as the afternoon advanced.

There we were, a hundred feet up, in the middle of a flat plain dotted with green, man-made humps of earth and gray, man-made ribbons of asphalt. Along the western horizon, we could see St. Louis, although we were too far away to pick out the Mississippi River. Closer at hand, there was a Wal-Mart. It seemed surreal.

"It was good to be the king," Rick commented as he turned the three-hundred-sixty degrees on his heel.

"No kidding," I said. "I'm glad humanity hasn't paved over every last bit of prehistory."

"Yeah." He glanced at his map again. "Where to next? Want to walk down to the woodhenge?"

"Sure. Why not?"

It was not quite a mile to the rebuilt woodhenge – a circle of posts that archaeologists say the Cahokians used to tell the time of year. "Getting anything here?" Rick asked me as we made the circuit around the poles.

"Nope," I said. "This was definitely not built by my people. We had more permanent and elaborate ways to tell time."

"Oh, la-de-da," Rick said, and I laughed with him. "Are we done? I'd like to get to the Arch before it closes."

So we headed back to the RV and the twenty-first century. "Need anything?" Rick asked as we passed the Wal-Mart. "Color TV? Bric-a-brac?"

I snorted. "It's just unbelievable that they put that thing there, bang up against all this history."

He shrugged. "Time marches on."

We made it to the Arch just in time. Ours was the last group to be admitted to a pod for the trek up the side of the giant structure. It felt a little claustrophobic following our afternoon in the open air, and we had to fight our way through the crowd to get to one of the tiny windows.

"Not bad, huh? And six times higher than we were at Cahokia," Rick said as we allowed ourselves to be elbowed aside.

I looked at him sidelong. "I think the Cahokians got the better end of the deal."

It was getting dark by the time we pulled out of the Arch complex, but we managed to find our RV park without a problem. "Thank goodness for Google Maps," Rick said as we set the leveling jacks for the night. "In the old days, we'd still be driving around."

"Maybe *you* would," I said loftily. "*My* sense of direction has always been excellent." I stood and dusted off my hands. "Do you remember which way the bathhouse is?"

Chapter 7

After supper – our first in the RV – we discussed our travel options. St. Louis was a hub where many interstates met, and two of them would get us to Los Angeles. I-70 was the more northerly route, through Kansas, Colorado, and Utah. "Lots of pretty country that way, once you get past Kansas. But then we'd be dropping south on I-15 through Las Vegas," Rick pointed out.

"Which we've previously discussed," I said, making a face. "What's our other option?"

"That would be I-44, which cuts through Missouri at an angle and meets up with I-40 in Oklahoma City."

Which, I recalled, was on Rick's original list. "Okay. Where's the tradeoff?"

He sat back. "You don't want to see the memorial?"

"Well, sure. But I thought I was going to pick a site to see, and then you'd pick one."

"I thought that would be just for when your buddies there dragged us off-course."

"Hmm." I fingered the effigies through my shirt. Needless to say, they were giving me no guidance; in fact, they'd mostly been quiescent through this first part of the trip. Maybe now that I was on the road, their job was mostly done. "That's not how I remember the deal, but all right. For now."

Rick threw me a metaphorical bone. "There's the National Petroglyph Monument in Albuquerque. That might be up their alley."

"Petroglyphs might be cool," I said, perking up.

"Old Town is kind of fun. We could have lunch there. Get some real Mexican food." He patted his belly and grinned. "But I don't have any other interest in Albuquerque – I've already done the tram up Sandia Mountain."

"It sounds like you're kind of sick of the place," I said. "When were you there?"

"Multiple times with the ex-wife. She has family there."

"Ah. We won't be looking them up, I gather."

"Not a chance."

The next few days featured a lot of driving and only a little site-seeing, but we did tick Oklahoma City off Rick's list.

The Oklahoma City National Memorial is as moving – and as sobering – as you would expect. It's built on the site where two men blew up a fertilizer-filled box truck outside the Murrah Federal Building in 1995. The explosion killed one-hundred-sixty-eight people, including nineteen children who were attending a daycare center in the building that day. Hundreds more were hurt. One of the perpetrators was executed for the crime; another was sentenced to life in prison.

We stayed later than we had planned, so we could see the chairs light up for the dead. "What were those guys thinking?" I said to Rick as we walked slowly along. "Those poor little kids."

"They were thinking the feds deserved payback for Waco," Rick reminded me. Two years before, federal authorities had surrounded the headquarters of a religious sect in Waco, Texas, and ended up firebombing the place. Seventy-five people died there.

"Revenge is so pointless," I said. "People shouldn't waste their time on it."

"I'll pass that along," Rick said.

I curled my lip at him. "I know there's no way to get people to understand that. But sooner or later, the bad guys get what's coming to them. It might not be for the thing you're upset about, but something will do them in."

"Like Gene?" he asked gently.

I let out a breath and nodded. "Yeah, like Gene. It took a long time for the Universe to get around to him, but it found him in the end." I'd heard from Bea earlier in the day; my ex-husband had waived extradition and was back in Maryland, at the state prison in Hagerstown. It would be quite some time before he would walk free again.

"How do you feel about that?" I'd asked her.

"To be honest, I'm relieved," she said. "I know for sure where he is. We won't be getting any more calls about him causing more trouble. And no more young girls will be at risk."

"I'm relieved about all of that, too," I said. "Do Tim and Emmy know?"

"I've emailed Tim. I thought you could call Emily."

My head came up. "Why?"

"You're going to be out there to visit her, aren't you?"

"Well, yeah, but we won't be arriving for a few days. I emailed her about that."

"Just call her, Mom," Bea said.

So I did. "Emily," I said. "How are you doing? How are classes going?"

"Oh, fine," she said vaguely. "It's commencement week, so it's a little crazy here on campus."

"It's still okay if we come to visit, right?" I asked. "We're on our way now."

"Right. I know that."

But she didn't say it was okay. "I'm sensing some reluctance," I said. "We don't have a firm arrival date yet – we can do some touring, maybe stop another couple of nights on the road, if that helps you. Or we could hang out at Abby and Sallie's if we're early."

"That's a brilliant idea," Em said immediately. "In fact, why don't you guys plan to do that anyway? My place is a mess, and I don't think I'll have time to clean before you get here."

"It's not like you have to put us up," I said, surprised by this pushback. Em was usually the kid I could count on to tell me what was what. Now she was suddenly coy.

"Yeah, I know," she said. "You've got the RV. Still, I think you'd be more comfortable making Aunt Abby's your home base."

"Well, okay," I said. "I'll talk to Abby and see. But I called you for another reason." And I told her about Gene.

"That's actually good news," she said, sounding more like the old Emily. "Bea's been frantic. Did she tell you Nana still won't get out of bed?"

I rolled my eyes. "She didn't mention it, but I'm not surprised to hear it."

"Mom," she said, "I know Nana's a drama queen, but Riley seems to think there's really something going on with her this time. And she won't go to the doctor."

"John could go to her, couldn't he? It's not like he doesn't know where she lives."

"I don't know." I thought she might say more, but suddenly there was a huge crash and a number of raised male voices.

"That sounded close," I said.

"Yeah," she said. She sounded scared.

"Emily?" I said sharply. "What's going on?"

"Nothing! Look, I've gotta go. I have class in fifteen minutes. Talk soon!" And she hung up on me.

I put away the phone and noticed Rick watching me. "What was that all about?"

"I wish I knew," I said.

He reached over and patted my knee. "You'll see her soon. Then we'll know everything."

I looked out the window. "I sure hope so. I'm tired of my kids keeping secrets from me. First Tim and that ridiculous story of him living overseas when he was in Florida the whole time. And now Emily." I looked at Rick. "How did I raise kids who won't tell me the truth?" And as soon as the words were out of my mouth, I remembered how long I'd pretended my marriage was perfect. "Never mind," I said with a sigh. "Forget I asked."

Rick barreled into Albuquerque on I-40 as if he had no intention of stopping. But we'd had an early start and a long day on the road, and we needed a break.

"Slow down, there, pardner," I said in my best faux Texas drawl.

"Now don't you worry yourself, little lady," he replied in something close to a John Wayne imitation. "I'm fixing to stop just as soon as I find a likely spot." He dropped the accent. "We need gas, if nothing else."

"I thought we were going to see the petroglyphs," I said.

"Oh. Right." He signaled to turn off the highway. "There's a Circle K up this way. Let's gas up there."

"We don't have to go at all, if you feel that strongly about it," I said.

He glanced at me as he slowed down to navigate the exit ramp. "To be honest, I'd rather keep heading west," he said. "The petroglyphs are small potatoes compared to the Grand Canyon. Have you ever seen it?"

"I've seen pictures. And on TV."

"Not the same. Not the same at all." He was silent as we drove the few blocks to the convenience store and pulled up at a gas pump. "Let's just stay overnight here and get back on the road in the morning. You'll like the Grand Canyon." He shot out of the RV and slammed the door.

"Okay for now, mister," I said to his reflection in the side mirror, "but this discussion isn't over."

By the time we'd found a campsite and settled ourselves for the night, I'd worked up a pretty good head of steam. I banged pots around on the stove, putting together a meal, while Rick went to the bathhouse to wash up. The RV had a bathroom, but we tended to use it only when stationary plumbing wasn't available.

When he came back in, I slammed our plates down on the table and sat down. He eyed his burger warily – the top bun had gone a little askew – and then looked at me the same way. "Maggie May?" he asked tentatively.

"Richard," I said.

He cringed, half joking. "Ouch."

I wasn't in the mood for it. Obviously. "I want some answers and I want them now," I said. "First you dangle petroglyphs in front of me, and then, when we get here, you dismiss the idea and lure me on with the Grand Canyon."

He raised one hand, thumb and forefinger pinched together, and looked at it quizzically.

"What are you doing?" I said, exasperated.

"I'm trying to figure out how one would dangle a petroglyph," he said.

"I'm counting to three," I said. "One…two…"

He folded his hands and plopped them beside his plate. "Yes, ma'am."

"You're derailing the discussion."

"I just don't see what the big deal is," he said, sitting back. "The petroglyphs…"

"Just stop it with the petroglyphs!" I said. "That's not the point."

"Then what *is* your point?"

"Why don't you want to set foot in Albuquerque?"

His shoulders slumped slightly. "It's Belinda." His ex-wife.

"I don't get it," I said. "You told me some of her relatives live here."

"No, *she* lives here," he said morosely.

"I thought she was still in Indy."

He sighed. "No. She and her new husband decamped for New Mexico right after the divorce was final. I don't want to run into her."

Now I understood what my job was. "How many people live in Albuquerque, Rick?"

He shrugged. "I don't know. Half a million people. Maybe more."

"And how big is it? How many square miles?"

He saw where I was going. "A lot," he said, nodding in resignation.

"Hundreds, maybe?"

"Not quite two hundred," he said. "But it's not just that it's unlikely we'd run into her. Everywhere I look here has some memory of her."

I watched him as he stared off into space. "Maybe this was a bad idea," I said quietly.

"What was?"

"Bringing you along. You're still in love with her."

His eyes met mine. "I'll always be in love with her, a little. But that doesn't mean I can't love someone else."

"Then make new memories here," I said. "Let's stay for a day. Let's do some of the things you've done before, and overwrite those memories with new ones."

"You're really jonesing to see those petroglyphs, aren't you?" he said with a small laugh.

"Yeah, and it's all your fault," I said, shaking my finger at him. "I wouldn't have known they were here if you hadn't brought them up. Now eat your supper before it gets cold."

"Yes, ma'am," he said. I balled up a paper napkin and tossed it at him.

It was early when we got to Petroglyph National Monument, but already hot. Rick piloted the RV to the Boca Negra Canyon parking area, where he said the trail was not only easy, but would provide optimal viewing opportunities of the primitive markings and figures scratched into the boulders. He said we could hike it in an hour or two, max. "And then we can get on the road," he said. "We should be able to make Flagstaff by nightfall."

I sighed inwardly and resolved to make sure he didn't rush me through this.

We hit the trail and I was instantly entranced. There were pictographs of birds, humans, and four-legged creatures, as well as spirals and other inscrutable designs. Rick said a park ranger had once told him the markings were a sort of road map on a route ancient Native Americans used from Mexico to Chaco Canyon. He said the local Indians had traditional teachings about the meanings of the glyphs, but they weren't willing to share them with outsiders.

"That's understandable," I said as we hiked a steep trail to the top of a cliff. "They probably don't want it commercialized. It's their spirituality, after all. Their way of life has been disrupted enough by the white man."

"Sure, but a lot of these were signposts," he said.

"Kilroy was here?" I said with a grin.

"More like Burma Shave signs," he replied. "Careful!" I was ahead of him on the trail, and a wobbly rock threw me off-balance. He grabbed my upper arm as I steadied myself.

"Thanks," I said, and kept moving.

A few minutes later, he asked, "You getting anything from your buddies?"

"No," I said. I pulled out the effigies and let them hang outside my t-shirt. "But then, the folks who migrated through here *really* weren't my people."

As if on cue, my bird lit up with a soft, golden glow. "Look there," Rick said quietly, stepping up beside me. "See it?"

It was impossible to miss. About ten feet ahead, a rock beside the trail sported the glyph of a bird – and it, too, was glowing golden.

"Thunderbird," I said, delighted. Then I glanced toward the north. "Look, Rick! There are more of them!"

"It's like they're pointing out the trail," he said. "That's really something."

I looked at my bird, whose glow had begun to fade. "What's up that way again?"

"Chaco Canyon. It's the ruins of a settlement built by the Anasazi, I think. They're pretty spectacular."

"Have you been there?" I looked up at him. "Can we go?"

"I thought we were going to the Grand Canyon."

I looked north wistfully. "And I want to get to Malibu to see Emily. I'm still worried about her after that phone call." I'd texted her after she hung up so abruptly, but I had yet to hear back from her.

"Tell you what," said Rick. "Let's keep moving west for now. We can catch Chaco and some of the other stuff up there on our way back."

There was no immediate complaint about that plan from either my bird or my turtle, so I agreed. "After all," I said as I dropped the necklace back inside my shirt, "it's not like those ruins are going anywhere."

As we continued up, I happened to glance toward the south — and stopped again. "Rick?" I said tentatively, pointing. "What are those?"

"Wow," he said. For stretching out in that direction, like pearls on a jagged cord, were rounded shapes glowing with a silvery light. "What are they? Moons? Or…"

"Not turtles," I said decisively. My turtle hadn't lit up. These were something else.

Rick clambered off the path toward the closest one. "This one has feet," he called.

"Feet?"

"Little legs."

I considered that. "How many?"

"Huh. Eight." He started back toward me. "They're spiders, I guess."

I squinted at the little lights as they faded out. "So the way north leads to the Thunderbird, and the way south leads to…Spider Woman?" I shook my head. "That doesn't make any sense. I'll have to do some research."

"Nobody around here believes in Spider Woman?" he asked.

"Well, yeah, of course. The Navajos say Spider Grandmother taught them how to weave. But their homeland is around here somewhere." I gestured vaguely at our surroundings. "Not south. South of here is Mexico."

"Could be the Mexican tribes have myths with similar themes," he said.

"I suppose," I said as I resumed climbing. "Tribes that came in contact with one another shared stories all the time. And crossing the Rio Grande was a lot easier then."

"No border guards," he agreed. "No fence."

"Exactly." I glanced back south. "I just wonder what it means."

Chapter 8

Interstate 40 shot west like an arrow through a landscape out of a science-fiction movie: desert on either side of the highway, with distant, wind-sculpted outcroppings in red, pink, tan, and black paralleling our route.

When we approached the turnoff for something called the Petrified Forest, I said, "Where's the forest?"

"Gone," Rick said. "Millennia ago. The trees fell into a river and were buried in sediment quickly enough that there was no oxygen to allow them to rot – so they sucked up minerals from the water instead. Now those tree trunks are basically rocks."

"Wow. Should we stop?"

"Up to you. You're the driver."

I weighed the time required to investigate petrified trees with my desire to get to Malibu. Malibu won. "We can stop on our way back," I said, and accelerated past the exit.

We can stop on our way back was fast becoming my mantra. The closer we got to the California state line, the more anxious I was to get to my daughter and find out what was going on with her. I still hadn't heard from her since that last phone conversation that had spooked me so badly.

But we were approaching the Grand Canyon, where Rick was itching to stop. To tell the truth, I was interested in seeing it, too. I'd been hearing all my life about what an amazing thing it was, and here we were, on its doorstep. So I took the exit off the interstate for Flagstaff and we started looking for a restaurant for dinner, as well as a place to park the RV for the night.

"You know what we could do," Rick said as we settled into a booth at a Mexican place. "We could drop south to Sedona."

"What's in Sedona?" I said.

"It's supposed to be a power vortex or something. Very New Agey." He pointed at my necklace, which I'd absently pulled out when we sat down. "Your buddies there might really like it."

My mouth quirked up at one corner. "They're not New Agey. You understand that part, right?"

"Oh, I know that. But it might be interesting to see whether they'd react to the supposed vortex. Given what happened in Albuquerque this morning."

I tucked the necklace back into its hiding place. "This isn't an experiment, you know."

"Sure, I know that." He looked up from his menu to see the stern look I was giving him. "I should shut up now, shouldn't I?"

"I'd recommend it." And we both went back to perusing our menus.

But now my interest was piqued. "How far is it to Sedona?" I asked as we left the restaurant, replete with a better dinner than I could have whipped up in the RV kitchen.

"Half an hour, maybe."

"Okay, sure."

The sun was dropping low as we headed south through the red-rock canyons. Rick drove so I could gawk. "John Ford lighting," I said. The movie director was famous for shooting scenes in the late afternoon to capture this golden light.

Rick nodded. "Let's stop here," he said, pointing to the first RV park we'd seen since leaving Flagstaff.

"You don't want to get closer to Sedona?"

He gave me a concerned look. "I'd like to, but this thing's driving a little funny. I'd rather get off the road now. See if the host at the camp here has any idea what might be wrong with it."

Immediately, I began to regret this detour. But I told myself it would be better to deal with whatever the problem was here, instead of ending up stuck with a broken-down RV on the side of the road in the middle of nowhere.

The host was very solicitous and offered to call his favorite mechanic in the morning. Not only that, but he handed us brochures for a couple of shuttle services that could pick us up and take us to Sedona. "Or even all the way to the Grand Canyon, if you haven't been there yet."

"It's on our itinerary," Rick said. "This is great news. Thanks so much for your help."

As we got back in the RV to find our campsite, I asked, "How long do you think this little pit stop will take?"

"No idea 'til the mechanic gets a look at it," he said.

The sun set quickly in the canyon, and the temperature dropped nearly as fast. I was glad I'd thought to bring a sweater.

Rick had taken a seat on the picnic bench at our site to catch the last of the light. He took one look at me as I climbed out of the RV, all bundled up, and laughed. "The desert doesn't agree with you, does it?" he said.

"I won't be settling down here, that's for sure. I don't think I could ever get used to these daily thirty-degree temperature swings," I said.

"I could build a fire, if you're that cold," he said.

"That's okay."

"There's a fire ring right here." He kicked at the metal ring on the ground next to the bench.

"No, I'm good."

"The guy's got firewood for sale in the office."

"Richard," I warned him.

He grinned and put an arm around me. I cuddled up next to him, grateful for more than the warmth.

The shuttle picked us up right on time the next morning That allowed us to spend a couple of hours poking around the stores in Sedona's quirky downtown: a cross between souvenir joints, upscale stores for the beautiful people, and the kinds of head shops I remembered from my college days.

Just for fun, I picked up a book about the local vortices. It included a map purporting to show their locations. "We'd need a car to get to any of them," I told Rick over the ice cream we'd bought in lieu of lunch.

"Maybe we could rent one," he said, and dug out his phone. "Oh, hey – I have voicemail from the mechanic." He listened to the message and put down the phone. "Looks like we lost a tie rod on the passenger side in the back," he said. "The guy says he should be able to have it fixed for us by the end of the day."

"That's a stroke of luck. I'd had visions of being stuck here for three or four days while he brought in a part from Phoenix or something." I scooped up the last of my Vanilla Vortex ice cream. I was disappointed; it didn't taste any different than regular vanilla.

"Must be the good vibes around here," he said with a smirk.

"Right," I said. "Let's see about renting a car. Now I want to see one of these vortexes in person."

"You can't *actually* see them, you know," he said loftily.

"Hush," I said, putting a finger to his lips. "You're harshing my vibe."

That got a laugh. "Okay. Let me call the mechanic back, and then we'll get a car."

Our first stop was Airport Mesa. It was crowded and noisy, from both people and planes, making it hard to concentrate. "Are you getting anything?" Rick asked.

"Nah. Maybe all the people are dampening the vibrations or whatever."

"Let's go someplace else, then." Rick closed his eyes, circled his finger over my map, and poked at it. Then he opened his eyes. "Cathedral Rock it is."

While he drove, I read the description in my book aloud. "'Cathedral Rock features an inflow vortex. Full of feminine energy, it's a good place to investigate negative emotions and past lives.'" Then I added, "We'll have to hike in. Looks like we have two options. The hike to the main site is more strenuous. The one to Buddha Beach is easier."

"Buddha Beach sounds promising," he said.

And it was – but not for me. For him.

Rick sank down onto the flat earth of Buddha Beach, surrounded by rock cairns left by others, closed his eyes, and cried. He didn't sob or blubber. It was just a continual flow of tears from the corners of his eyes.

I moved some distance away to give him privacy, and took out my necklaces. Then I sat down, closed my eyes, and waited.

Nothing.

I sighed and opened my eyes again. This land wasn't mine, these spirits weren't mine, and the longer I sat here, the more anxious I was to get back on the road. I began to feel angry at Rick for suggesting that we stop here in the first place. We could have stayed in Flagstaff and driven up to the Grand Canyon today. But no – he had to drag me to Sedona. Now the RV needed repairs, and we were spending tons of money on a rental car and extra nights on the road – and for what? So he could sit on a rock and cry?

That's when I realized the vortex energy was amplifying my anxiety. I'd brought the wrong kind of energy to this place; instead of being open to the experience, I'd closed myself off with my busy, unproductive thoughts.

I forced myself to clear my mind and breathe. In, out, in, out. The familiar rhythm calmed me. And while I received no additional insights to my situation or the tasks that lay before me, at least I was able to return to Rick with a lighter spirit and a much less accusatory attitude.

Maybe Sedona had been good for me, after all.

Rick was silent during the drive back. But that night, in our bed in the dark, he was fully present – in a way that he had never been up to that point in our relationship. He didn't say anything about what he'd experienced at Buddha Beach, but I had to assume he'd wrestled with a demon or two left over from his marriage – and it sure seemed to me as if he'd won the round.

The mechanic was not only efficient, but cheap. By the time we returned to camp, the RV was fixed and deemed road-worthy again, and our wallets weren't that much lighter. We hadn't yet turned in the rental car, so we decided to take it to the Grand Canyon and leave the gas hog at the RV park.

Probably hundreds of thousands of words have been written, and hundreds of thousands of photos have been taken, of the Grand Canyon – but none truly do it justice, so I'm not going to try to do it here. The West is rife with canyons cut by water and wind over millennia. What makes the Grand Canyon special is its sheer size. The vista, the colors, the changing clouds and distant rainbows, all contribute to a three-hundred-sixty-degree delight to the senses.

We'd been meandering from one part of the overlook to another for maybe half an hour when Rick said, "Want to go down into the canyon?"

I looked at him as if he'd grown another head. "You're kidding, right?"

"We don't have to hike. We could rent mules."

"No, thank you. I'm good right here." I turned back to the view. A moment later, I turned back to Rick. "Did *you* want to go down into the canyon?"

"Me? No. I've already done it. I just thought you might want to go."

"Were you with Belinda?" I ventured.

He didn't wince when I said her name, which I took as a good sign. "No, this was before that. I had a summer job with the Park Service between my sophomore and junior years at I.U. Some of my buddies talked me into hiking the canyon with them." He gazed down into the canyon. "I was in a lot better shape then."

"We all were," I said with a laugh. "How was the hike?"

"Going down was a piece of cake," he said.

"And coming up?"

He squinted at me. "Let's just say it took a lot longer."

We stopped in Flagstaff for supper on our way back to the RV. Since I had a decent phone signal, I thought I'd try Emily once more.

Still no answer. I left her a voicemail, letting her know we were leaving Sedona in the morning and hoped to meet her for supper the next day – my treat.

"That doesn't sound promising," Rick said as I ended the call.

"No, it doesn't." I sighed and put the phone on the table next to me. "This is very unlike her. Tim's the one who dodges my calls. Not Em." And Tim had been much better about returning calls once he came clean about where he was living. He'd been telling me for years that he was backpacking around Europe, but it turned out he'd been working in Mexico, teaching English as a second language. And he'd met a girl named Ana – who, the last I knew, was recovering from injuries she'd suffered in an accident in Mexico City. Tim had rushed off from Rockville to be with her. I'd received a couple of emails from him, but nothing for a week or so.

Come to think of it, when Tim was living with Ana's brother in Florida and waiting for his work visa to be renewed, Emmy had covered for him. She hadn't dodged my calls, but she'd usually been too busy to talk. Or so she'd claimed.

"Maybe I should call Tim," I said at this point in my ruminations. "Maybe he's heard from her."

"Why Tim?" Rick asked. "Doesn't Abby live nearby? I mean, if Emily's in trouble, it would be better to ask someone who's close enough to check on her."

My eyes sprang wide open. *In trouble?* The thought had not occurred to me. "Yeah. I should talk to Abby. She needs to know our plans anyway." I was already punching up her number on my phone.

My ex-sister-in-law, bless her, was *not* dodging my calls. "Maggie!" she sang out. "When are you getting here? Please say it's soon."

"Why?" I said.

"Because I miss your face. Why else?"

So I told her about Emmy. "Have you heard from her?"

"No. And I'm sure she'd call us if she were in trouble. Tell Rick to stop making you crazy."

"You can tell him yourself tomorrow," I said. "We're in Flagstaff right now. We should be in L.A. by suppertime tomorrow."

"Okay, so Maggie? Here on the West Coast, we call it dinner." She was laughing at me.

"Fine, whatever. Give me your address again. I'll call you when we're close."

She rattled it off, and then said, "You guys leave everything to Sallie and me. We'll get hold of Emily and make sure she's here when you get here."

"Thanks, Abby."

"No need to thank me," she said. "What are sisters for?"

Chapter 9

It took somewhat longer to cross the desert than we'd expected, largely because the RV kept threatening to overheat. We stopped repeatedly to let the engine cool off a little – a pipe dream, given that the temperature had soared past 100 by mid-morning. At one point, Rick turned off the air conditioning and opened as many windows as we could, just to give the engine a break. We drank what seemed like gallons of water and I was still thirsty.

"So am I," Rick yelled over the road noise. "You can't tell you're sweating – the air's so dry it's evaporating."

"You're kidding," I yelled back.

He shook his head. "Nope. Keep the water coming," he said.

We stopped for lunch at a rest area west of Needles. The interior of the building housing the restrooms felt like a meat locker, after the portable sauna we'd been driving in. "Can we just stay here for a few hours?" I suggested. "Just 'til the sun goes down."

"I hear you," Rick said. "But we have dinner plans in Whittier."

"Right." I pushed myself upright. "Let me drink another gallon of water before we get back on the road."

A few hours later, we were cruising down the 610 Freeway, as I learned the Angelenos call it. Los Angeles looked like every major metropolitan area I'd ever been in, except for the nods here and there to Spanish Revival architecture: buildings covered in fake adobe, with red-tiled roofs and elaborate plastered trim.

Before Abby and Sallie bought their home in Whittier, the only thing I knew about it was that President Nixon had grown up there. I'd vaguely recalled that he'd been brought up as a Quaker. In fact, Whittier was founded by Quakers.

The city still had a friendly, peaceful vibe, with a real downtown, a liberal arts college, and several residential areas marked as historic districts.

It all felt very familiar; I might have believed I was in Indiana, except for the distant mountains we had crossed just a short time before.

Abby and Sallie had bought a renovated 1940s-era home near Central Park. We found a spot for the rig on the street, down the block from their home.

"Welcome!" Abby said, answering the door with Bernice perched on one hip. "Can you say hello, Bernice?"

The last time we'd seen the baby, she couldn't even turn over yet. Now, six months later, she was a sturdy thing with her hair in a topknot and her fingers in her mouth. She looked away from us at first, then turned back and smiled, ducking her head against Abby's shoulder.

"You flirt," Abby said as we laughed. Then she gave us each a one-armed hug. "The place is a mess, but come on in."

"It's fine," I said, glancing around as we entered. "Is Sallie home yet?"

At that moment, Emmy poked her head into the doorway at the end of the hall. "Mom!" she called, and came straight into my arms.

I sucked back sudden tears. I hadn't allowed myself to acknowledge exactly how worried I'd been until I saw her. Then it all surfaced. "Emmy," I whispered. Then I leaned back, still holding onto her. "Why didn't you ever answer your phone? I've been calling you…"

She grimaced. "My phone got stolen. I didn't have time to get a new one until today." She stepped out of my embrace. "You must be Rick."

He held out his hand and they shook. "And you must be Emily. I've heard so much about you."

Em gave me the side-eye and laughed. "I bet you have. But was it, 'I've heard *so* much about you!'" – this she said in a chirpy tone – "or, 'I've heard about *you*'" – which she delivered with a knowing wink.

"Neither one," he said. "It was more like, 'Oh, that Emmy…'" He put the back of one hand to his brow.

"It was not," I said with mock indignance, as everyone else laughed.

"Yep, that's Mom, all right," Emmy said. She reached for Bernice, who had begun to babble as if joining in the conversation, and started back down the hall. "Come on. The great room is this way."

Abby's phone chirped. "Be right there," she said, and detoured into another room.

The great room was decorated in sage green and bronze. Windows showcasing the mountain view, together with a fireplace, dominated one wall. The left-hand third of the room was kitted out as a dining room; a sleek table and chairs sat below a modern light fixture. The rest of the room contained comfortable seating, with brightly-colored toys stashed in the far corner. Rick and I sank down into a loveseat covered in a plush fabric.

"How was the drive?" Em asked.

"A little dicey," Rick admitted. "The RV kept trying to overheat. I'd like to have someone take a look at it while we're here."

"It'll need to be in tip-top shape for the trip to Mexico," I said, not thinking.

Em perched on an ottoman and dropped the baby onto her blanket on the floor. "You don't mean to *drive* all the way down to see Tim, do you?" she asked.

I glanced between her and Rick. "Maybe," I hedged.

"Mom," Emmy said, "that is an outrageously bad idea. In fact, I can't even begin to tell you what a bad idea that is. Haven't you heard about all the murders?"

"I know there's been a lot of drug-related violence," I said, "but we wouldn't be driving anywhere near there, would we?"

Emmy's mouth dropped open. "No, of course not. Only *right through the middle of it.*"

"But they wouldn't kill tourists, would they?"

Em might have begun insulting my intelligence next, but Abby chose that moment to walk through the door. "That was Sallie on the phone," she said. "She's just leaving the hospital. She'll be home in about fifteen minutes." She made a face at the baby and clapped her hands. "I'm a terrible hostess. Anybody thirsty?"

"Yes," Rick and I chorused.

The conversation drifted to other topics, which I was glad about. I still meant to drive to Mexico, and I knew Rick and I were headed for a showdown over it. But I wasn't in the mood for it that night.

Supper – sorry, *dinner* – was salmon with a delicate citrusy glaze. Bernice sat with us in her high chair, her fingers making little pink crumbs of her salmon. Sallie made sure some of it eventually got into her mouth.

"So are you teaching any summer classes?" I asked Em.

She checked her water glass halfway to her mouth. Her eyes darted between me and Abby. Then she took a sip and put her glass down. "No. I'm taking the summer off to work on my dissertation. I thought I'd told you that."

"And she'll be working," Abby said, nodding at my daughter. Warning her, maybe?

"Right, yeah," Emmy said, warming to the topic. "I've been hired by a start-up in Simi Valley to design their back-end systems. My dissertation adviser is friends with the owner of the company – that's how they got my name."

"Wonderful," I said. "Sounds like it's right up your alley."

Rick frowned. "Is it salaried, or…?"

"I'm a consultant," Em said.

"And how are they compensating you?"

Em smiled sardonically. "It's not an unpaid internship, if that's what you're asking. I have a contract."

"And you had a lawyer go over this contract?"

"Rick," I said, laying a hand on his.

"No, this is important," he told me. "I don't want to see her taken advantage of." He looked at her. "Have you signed it yet?"

"No." She shrugged. "You can look at it. I don't care. I did have a friend who's in law school look it over, but another pair of eyes can't hurt."

"The only real problem is going to be getting up there," Sallie said. "Good salmon, Abby. I like this recipe."

"I'm glad. I found it in that cookbook of your mother's." They exchanged a smile.

I was still stuck on Em's transportation issues. "Don't you have a car?" I asked her. "I thought everybody in southern California had to have a car."

"I *had* a car," she said. "It got stolen along with my phone."

"Oh, no," I said. "What can we do to help?"

"Nothing, Mom," Emmy said. There was that defensive tone again.

"How are you getting home tonight? We can give you a ride," I said.

"No! I mean, I'm taking the bus," she amended.

I looked again at my middle child. Emily had always been the most blunt-spoken of my three children. Always said what was on her mind. No subterfuge.

I pushed away from the table and stood. "I think I'd like to go out back and see your garden, ladies. Is that okay?"

Abby and Sallie exchanged a glance. "Sure," said Abby. "The door's right there." She indicated French doors on the same wall as the fireplace.

"Come on, Em," I said. "Let's go check it out."

She tossed her napkin on the table the same way she had as a teenager when she was sure she was about to be punished. I half expected her to roll her eyes, too. But she rounded the table readily enough and met me at the doors.

To tell the truth, there wasn't much to see in Abby and Sallie's backyard. A stockade fence offered privacy and a place to hang a wind chime; otherwise it was mostly grass, with a concrete patio sporting a couple of plastic chairs that had seen better days. "Sallie keeps saying she's going to plant flowers," Em said, surveying the yard. "But she works, like, a billion hours a week."

I sat down gingerly on one of the chairs, then slid back as it proved sturdy enough to hold my weight. "Em," I said. "Come on, tell me. What's going on?"

She sagged into the other chair and leaned forward, her arms dangling awkwardly between her knees. Then she drew in a breath and sat up. "I'm not working on my dissertation," she said.

I paused. "You're taking some time off?" I asked. "Or..."

"No. I quit the program."

"You dropped out of school?" I asked. "Why?"

She barked a laugh. "It's not really *dropping out* when you're in grad school." She sighed. "But yeah, I guess that's one way to look at it. I dropped out."

"Why?" I said again.

"I lost interest." She looked away, over the fence and to the mountains beyond.

"And what made you lose interest?" I kept my voice level, even thought I wanted to shake her and make her tell me faster. *Come on, Emily. Quit stalling.*

"I...my..." She shook her head. "Fuck it. Just say it, Em." She looked straight at me. "I had a relationship with my adviser, and the university found out and got rid of both of us."

I maintained my poker face. "He was violating some kind of ethical rule?" I said. "Was that it?"

"Yeah."

"Why couldn't you just get another adviser?"

"Because they decided they couldn't be sure how much of the work was mine and how much was Tahir's." Her eyes were hard. "It was *all* my work, Mom. He hadn't even been advising me much toward the end."

"Where is he?"

She sighed. "He went back to Pakistan. But he found me this consulting job before he left. They wouldn't hire me outright because I don't have a doctorate. The owner of the company is basically taking me on as a favor to Tahir."

I asked quietly, "Do you love him?"

She glanced at me. "Not enough to follow him to Pakistan and become one of his sister-wives or whatever."

I breathed a little easier. I'd been worried she would move halfway around the world from me. "What about transferring to another university? Could you take your research and all the work you've done up to now, and enroll at another school to finish up?"

She cocked head and looked heavenward. "I mean, maybe. If I prove myself at this job, I'll have a better shot at it."

"Well, that's something." Then a thought occurred to me. "You had to leave campus, didn't you? You can't live in student housing if you're not a student."

"Yeah. And the only thing I could afford was a dump in San Pedro." She looked at me, scared. "Those guys you heard arguing while we were on the phone the other day? That was a drug deal gone bad. That stuff happens all the time in my neighborhood. Homeless guys sleep on our porch every night. I have to step over them if I come in late. The place smells like an outhouse because they pee on our fence. My car was stolen when I left it unlocked while I brought in some groceries." There were tears in her eyes. "I need to move, but I don't have the money to do it."

"And you need a new car," I said.

She sighed and swiped at her eyes with the heel of her hand. "The insurance hadn't yet lapsed, thank goodness, so I'll get money for the car. But I need to find another place to live."

I got up and held out my arms, and she readily moved into them.

"When do you start the new job?" I asked.

"Week after next."

"Okay. I'll see what I can do."

"You want to rescue her," Rick said as we bedded down in Sallie and Abby's guest room that night.

I paused. "I want to *help* her. There's a difference."

"Only semantically."

I glowered at him. "She needs to get out of that apartment."

"I understand that."

"We can at least help her move," I said.

"Sure. This month. And next month she'll need money for something else."

I shook my head. "No, Rick. This is Emily. She's not a spendthrift."

He lifted one shoulder. "Maybe. Maybe not. But I know one thing, Maggie May: you're not made of money." He tapped my chin lightly with a forefinger to emphasize each of his last few words. Then he leaned back against the headboard. "I want to look over this contract she's being offered. Sometimes 'consultant' is a fancy word for 'we're too cheap to give you benefits.' Maybe it'll be okay and it'll turn out I'm worried for nothing. But I want to make sure they're not taking advantage of her." He looked hard at me. "For *your* peace of mind."

"I appreciate that." I smiled. "And we can help her with first and last month's rent."

"And that's it," Rick said. "No more."

I sat up and looked hard at him. "What is your problem, Rick? Why are you so concerned about the help I want to give my children?"

He let out a breath. "Because your children know you just got money from your mother's estate."

"And you think they'll want to help me spend it." It wasn't a question.

"Of course they will," he said. "Come on, Maggie May. I'm sure you've read stories about people who win the lottery. They get besieged by long-lost relatives and so-called friends they haven't spoken to in years."

"But that's…" I stopped. I'd been about to say that was different, and my kids would never be like that. But I realized all those lottery winners had thought the same thing.

"I understand the desire to help the people you love," he said.

"I know you do," I broke in with a laugh. "You were all set to help me buy a bigger motor home."

He grinned sheepishly. "Touché, Maggie May."

Chapter 10

Sallie had to work the next day, but Abby had taken time off to hang out with us. She alternated between taking care of the baby and advising Rick on where to take the RV for service. It was my RV and it should have been me taking it in. But he'd stepped into the role of Mr. Fixit while we were in Sedona, and that had worked out okay. "Men like dealing with other men when it comes to cars," he'd told me at some point the day before. "They think women don't know anything about mechanical stuff."

"In my case, they're right," I said. "But neither do you."

He tipped an imaginary cap to me. "But I can talk the lingo."

I rolled my eyes and decided to let him play his game. It was to my advantage in this instance, anyway. While he was busy with the RV, I intended to spend some time helping to get Emily squared away.

A lot of the finesse of parenting is knowing when to let your kids try and fail, and when to butt in and help. It's true when they're learning to walk – do you pad the corners of the coffee table, or do you let them clunk their heads a few times? It's true when they're teenagers, too – how much supervision do you give them and their friends?

Once they've become adults, it's tempting to think your parenting days are over. But they're not. And the hardest thing about parenting young adults is standing back and watching them make their own mistakes. You have to keep reminding yourself that you had to make your own mistakes, too. After all, failure is the best teacher.

But sometimes you just can't resist. And that's where I found myself with Emily's situation. So I called a taxi and set off to see her in her native habitat.

San Pedro is a beach town, with the ubiquitous southern California palm trees and a couple of museums along the waterfront. But it's also right on the harbor, across from the very industrial docks at Long Beach. One of the big attractions in San Pedro is the U.S.S. Iowa, a decommissioned battleship docked permanently on the waterfront. In short, it's a gritty little town.

Emmy's apartment building was several blocks from the beach. It looked like it might have been a motel once, with that shared, long, covered walkway that ran the length of the building. I winced when I saw it; it reminded me a little too forcefully of the no-tell motel I'd landed in after Mom's house burned down.

Then again, Emmy's life had gone up in flames, too, in a way.

I stepped to her door and knocked. She used the peephole first, and then yanked the door open, her mouth an O of shock. "Mom! What are you doing here?"

"Can I come in?" I asked pleasantly.

"Um, yeah, I guess. Sure." Her eyes darted past me, searching the street in front of the building. "Where did you park? You didn't bring the RV, did you?"

"No, I took a taxi. Rick's taking the rig in for service."

"Oh, that's right." She relaxed a little. "Come on in."

The interior also reminded me of the no-tell motel. It was an efficiency, with a tiny kitchenette across from a bed with a sagging mattress. A TV sat on a mottled metal stand, but I assumed it didn't work, as Emmy had draped underwear over it to dry. She snatched up her undies and stuffed them in an adjacent drawer. "Have a seat," she said. "Oh." She scooted a pile of papers – mail, maybe, and other printed materials – off the seat of an armchair in the corner by the window. "There you go. Want something to drink?"

"How long have you been living here?" I said as I sat.

She curled her lip as she perched on the edge of the bed. "Since before Thanksgiving."

"So when you were so busy with finals and things," I said slowly, "when I was trying to get hold of Tim to come and help with Nana…?"

"My life was in shambles, yeah." She looked down. "I'm not proud of that. I just didn't have the bandwidth to deal with everything at once."

"No apology necessary." I stood. "So. What can I do to help?"

I could almost see the word *nothing* form on her lips. Then she shut her mouth tightly. When she opened it again, she said, "I need to get all my financial stuff done this week. So whatever you can do…"

"We can certainly take you car shopping," I said. "Do you have a letter from your insurance company or something?"

"Oh!" She bounced up and grabbed her phone. "They sent me an email. I saw it when I set up my email account on this phone this morning, but I forgot to open it." She punched it up and sat back down with a relieved smile. "They're depositing the money straight into my checking account. I should have access to it tomorrow."

"That's quick work," I said, thinking of the weeks I waited for Mom's homeowner's insurance company to pay out after the fire. "I think I want to switch to your car insurance."

"So we could go look at cars later in the week," she said. "To be honest, I'd rather be moved into a new place before I drive it off the lot."

"I can't imagine why," I said. "So the very first order of business, then, is to find you a new place to live."

"That would be spectacular," Emmy said with a bright smile.

Abby picked us up, and we headed north to Simi Valley. I sat in the back seat with Bernice so Em could direct Abby.

By the time we stopped for lunch, we had toured several places, and Em had filled out applications for two of them. "Now, we wait, I guess," she said, digging into her salad.

For a moment, I watched Bernice play with the bits of food Abby had given her to eat. Something had been bothering me for the past couple of hours. Maybe Rick's suspicious mind was rubbing off on me, but I figured it wouldn't hurt to check. "Emily," I said, and her head came up. "Who's paying for the place where you're living now?"

She glanced at Abby, swallowed, and said, "I am."

"But where's the money coming from? You're not working, are you?"

"I had the last paycheck from teaching before the university let me go…"

"But you've been out of school for at least six months," I said. "And I know teaching doesn't pay that well. A couple of days ago, you bought a new phone. Now you're buying a new car."

"I told you, I had insurance for the car."

"And for the phone, too?"

She glanced again at Abby. "Nana's helping me."

My eyebrows shot up. "You're getting money from your grandmother?" This was completely unlike the Ruth I knew.

"Yeah." She cut another look at Abby, who was studying her own salad.

"Okay. Both of you, look at me." Both pairs of eyes were trained on me. To Abby, I said, "Why does she keep looking at you?"

She sighed. "It's not Mom who's sending her the money. It's Riley."

That seemed more plausible, but still. "Then why the subterfuge?"

Emily took a deep breath and let it out. "Because I thought you'd be mad if you knew I was getting money from Dad."

"Okay, wait," I said. "First the money was coming from Nana, and then Riley, and now you're telling me your father is sending you cash." I leaned forward. "Which is it?"

"It's Dad," she said. "But Riley's made all the arrangements because of course Dad hasn't been in a place where he could set any of this up."

"I'll buy that," I said. "But why drag Nana into it?"

"I already told you. Because I thought you'd be mad if I told you Dad was giving me money."

I shook my head. "Okay. For the record, Emily, I don't care who's bankrolling you, as long as it's not coming from some illegal source." I sighed and sat back. "I was afraid you were selling drugs. Or selling your body."

"Mom!" Emmy said, shocked.

"Well, I had no way of knowing what was going on," I said.

"You really think I would do that?"

"No, honey, but…"

Emmy slid her chair back. Its metal feet squealed on the concrete floor. "I need some air," she said, and fled.

"Nicely done," Abby commented as she took another forkful of salad.

I rounded on her. "Why didn't *you* tell me what was going on?"

She put down her fork. "It's not like you haven't had your own stuff to deal with over the past few months. We were trying not to complicate your life any more than it already was."

"Thanks. I think." I sipped my iced tea. Then I lowered my voice and asked, "How much is he sending her?"

"A couple of thousand a month," she said. "Which sounds like a lot, but it barely covers her rent and groceries. L.A. is expensive."

"I guess it is. Who bought her the phone?"

"Sallie and I did." She paused. "We didn't drop a ton on it. It's refurbished."

"Yeah, okay." I sighed. "Well, thank you for taking care of my kid when I couldn't."

"She's not a kid," Abby said. "She's a young woman, Maggie. She's smart and resourceful, and she'll be fine once she gets back on her feet." She sipped her own drink. "We met Tahir, you know."

"Oh?" She had my attention. "What did you think?"

"You want to know the truth?" she said. She glanced around for any sign of Emmy. Then she said, "We figured he was angling to get her to marry him so he could stay here legally. Em told us he'd already overstayed his work visa. Neither of us was surprised when he was deported."

I considered that. "No wonder she wants no part of him now. Poor Em." I looked toward the door. "Was she really kicked out of her program?"

Abby lifted a shoulder. "That's what she says. Sallie thinks she left voluntarily – too many memories. Personally, I think she's too embarrassed to show her face on campus again."

"Hmm," I said. Abby's assessment sounded more like the Em I knew.

Bernice took that moment to decide she'd had enough, and burst into tears. "Oh, punkin'," Abby said. She wiped the baby's hands, further upsetting her, and hauled her out of her high chair for a cuddle.

I pushed my own chair back and stood. "I'm going to go find Emmy and apologize. Then we can get going."

Em wasn't hard to find – she was sitting on a bench outside the restaurant. She didn't acknowledge me as I sat next to her, but I didn't expect her to. "Your mother," I said, "has a habit of saying stupid stuff when she ought to keep her mouth shut."

She glanced at me. "No kidding."

"I never meant to imply…"

She waved it away. "I know. It's fine." She let out a sigh. "This year has just been so *hard*."

"I know," I said.

"First Nana being so sick, and then Grandma going bonkers, and her and Uncle Sandy dying in the fire. And then *Lenny*." The half-brother her father had gotten on his and Abby's older sister.

"Lee," I said. Ruth called him Lenny, but his adoptive parents called him Lee.

"Right, Lee. I know." She looked at me. "And I've been out here, away from it all. You were right in the middle of it. How are you even upright, Mom? How do you get up every day?"

I felt a tiny thump against my breastbone – the first one I'd felt in quite a while. I drew out my necklace and held the effigies out toward her.

She glanced at my face, searching, and then reached a finger out to touch the turtle. "I remember this one," she said.

"Tim told me the two of you would sneak it out and play with it sometimes."

She smiled, remembering. "One time it hopped across the room by itself. Scared us shitless." She fingered the bird. "This one's new. Where'd it come from?"

"My burial mound," I said, watching her carefully.

Her reaction didn't disappoint. "What?"

I filled her in on my first meeting with Granny and Zed, the charge Granny had given me to renew the Earth by helping more than a thousand people, and the discovery of the bird effigy near where Hopewell-era Maggie had been buried.

"Does Rick know about all this?" she asked.

"Some of it. And he's seen me in action, as it were. The spirits tied to these effigies led us to the guy who was selling the RV."

She gave me a skeptical look. "Seriously?"

"Feel free to ask him about it. Actually, I think that was the point when he became a believer."

She let the necklace drop and sat quietly for a moment, her hands in her lap. At last, she said, "So you think I'm one of the people you need to help?"

"Why not?" I said. "I've meddled in the lives of everybody else in this family. Might as well get involved in yours, too."

She laughed and held out her hand. "Okay."

I put my hand in hers and squeezed. "But only first and last month's rent," I warned.

She laughed again. "That's all I'll need. Thanks, Mom."

After dinner the next night, Rick sat before the unlit fireplace, going over Emmy's contract, while Sallie, Emmy, and I cleared the table and chatted in the kitchen. Abby had taken the baby upstairs for her bath. Every now and then, I could hear Bernice's happy splashing in the tub.

Emmy had been accepted by the apartment complex she'd liked the best, and we were discussing logistics to get her moved in before Rick and I got back on the road at the end of the week. The RV dealer had swapped out some parts and "summerized" our rig so it wouldn't overheat in the desert again. It hadn't dawned on either Rick or me that the previous owner had mostly used it in winter, and that the engine might need to be tweaked for desert travel. The dealer said we weren't the first people he'd ever seen to make that mistake — and we wouldn't be the last, either.

Presently, Rick joined us in the kitchen. He handed the contract back to Emmy and said, "I'm impressed. I half-expected it to be a dog's breakfast, but whoever wrote it made it fair to both parties. There are a couple of things I would have done differently, but neither would make a material change."

"So you think I should sign it?" Emmy said.

"Absolutely."

She grinned from ear to ear. "Anybody got a pen?"

A couple of days later, we helped Em move into her new place. She called some of her friends, too, which was a good thing, as we all had old knees and Em's new place didn't have an elevator.

That evening, we celebrated with the traditional beer and pizza amid boxes and bags at Emmy's new place. "This is the nicest apartment I've ever had," she said. "Thanks, everyone. I really feel like my life is turning around. Finally!"

We laughed and toasted her.

"And I'm going to pay all of you back," she said. "For the phone, and the rent deposit, and everything."

"No worries, Emily," Sallie said. "The phone was a gift."

"And I appreciate it, Aunt Sallie," she said, "but that's not how I was raised." She grinned at me.

I grinned back, as my turtle and bird warmed my skin under my shirt. I could almost feel more of the tarnish on my turtle melting away.

Chapter 11

We said goodbye to Abby, Sallie, and Bernice after dinner the following evening. Even after the RV dealer had given us the all-clear, Rick was leery about driving across the Mojave Desert during the heat of the day. So we napped that afternoon and planned to drive all night. Rick had consulted the map and his GPS app, and concluded it would take us a little over ten hours to drive back to the Four Corners area. If one of us napped while the other was driving, he reasoned, we could be there by breakfast time.

"Why are we going back on I-40?" I asked. I pulled the map toward me and pointed to Interstate 10, farther south. "Wouldn't it make more sense to go that way, if we're heading for Mexico?"

"I thought you wanted to go to Chaco Canyon," Rick said. "Remember the thunderbird petroglyphs lighting the way?"

"Of course I do," I said. "But the spider petroglyphs were pointing the *other* way."

"And aren't you supposed to contact somebody for Granny when you get to the Four Corners?" he went on reasonably.

I was beginning to hate that tone of voice. It always meant he was right. "Fine," I said grudgingly. "Let's go to Chaco."

So it was that we rolled into Gallup, New Mexico, at sunrise the following morning on next-to-no sleep. We found an open diner, parked the rig, and went inside for coffee.

"How far is it from here to Chaco Canyon?" Rick asked the waitress as she filled our mugs.

She nodded out the window at our RV. "You folks come here in that?"

"Yeah," I said. "Why?"

"I wouldn't drive it to Chaco," she said. "The last ten miles are dirt, and nothing but ruts." She pointed her lips toward a rack of brochures by the door. "We've got some contact information over there for folks who run jeep tours. All of them are reliable. You'd be better off calling one of them, seeing if they can take you out there in the next day or two. I'll let you have another minute with the menu."

We looked at each other in dismay as she bustled off. "Did you know that?" I asked Rick.

He shrugged. "I'd read about it, but I thought they just put it in there to scare people into spending money on a tour. I figured we'd be okay."

"She didn't look like a shill for a tour company," I said. "Let me call Granny's contact. Maybe they can tell us what to do next."

I dug through my purse to find the slip of paper Janie McClatchey had given me at Cahokia. Unearthing it at last, I pulled out my phone and punched in the number on the paper on the keypad.

On the other side of the diner, a phone rang. "Hello?" a high tenor voice said, live in the diner and a beat later on my phone.

I began to laugh. "I should have known." I raised my hand high above my head. "See the woman waving across the room from you?"

Now he began to laugh. "Yeah, I see you. I'll be right over."

Rick was smiling in disbelief. "He's here?"

"Yeah. Here he comes." I scooted over so our contact could sit down in our booth. He was maybe in his early forties and built like a linebacker – tall and broad-shouldered. He wore a Western-style shirt with pearl snaps and well-worn jeans, and his straight black hair hung in a thick braid down his back.

"You must be friends of Granny's," he said, in that voice that belied his size. "I'm Randy Deschine."

"I'm Maggie Brandt," I said, "and this is my friend Rick Hughes. Please, join us." I motioned to the empty place beside me.

"Oh, no, thank you. My coffee is getting cold over there. I just came to say hello."

"Well, all right," I said. "We won't keep you. But we're looking for a ride to Chaco Canyon today, and I thought you might know of someone. We've been told the road is no good for RVs."

"That's right," he said. "It's not. I can take you up there."

"We'd hate to impose," Rick said.

"You're not imposing at all," Randy said. "You folks take your time with your breakfast, and when you're done, we'll get started."

"How much do you charge?" Rick asked.

"Oh, no, man," Randy said with a laugh. "For friends of Granny's, it's free. I'll see you in a few minutes." And he loped off across the diner to his own table.

Rick leaned toward me. "Do you think we should trust him?"

"Granny hasn't steered me wrong yet," I said.

Randy's ride was a pickup truck that had seen better days. "Hop in," he said, scooping up a handful of papers and dropping them into the back seat. "Sorry it's a mess. I didn't have time to clean up." I took the middle seat, between the two men.

"Will the RV be okay here?" asked Rick as he got in.

"Oh, sure," said Randy. "The owners are used to running interference on tourists."

"Hmph," said Rick. Privately, I agreed with him. I knew we were tourists, of course, but I had this fantasy that we were special because of our association with Granny. Randy didn't seem to think so, though.

"Is this your line of work?" I asked Randy. "I mean, do you often take tourists up to Chaco?"

"Sometimes," he said, and put the truck in gear.

As we roared out of the parking lot, Rick and I traded a look that said, *What are we getting ourselves into?* The question was academic at that point; the diner was quickly receding behind us.

I turned back to our chauffeur. "So did you just happen to be there this morning, or were you waiting for us?"

"A little bit of both," he said. "I talked to Zed a couple of days ago, and he told me you were on your way. But I didn't know when you'd get here."

That didn't surprise me, given that we were playing our itinerary by ear. "Was Granny with him?" I asked. "How is she?"

"Fine, from what he said. She's tolerating the chemo pretty well for someone her age. He said the doctors weren't keen on being too aggressive with her treatment – given that she's so old, and all. But he said she had a little talk with them, and made sure they understood how important it was that she get over this."

"What does her age have to do with it?" I asked. When Ruth had been treated for uterine cancer, the subject had never come up.

"It's a question of quality of life," said Rick. "I saw it with some of the seniors in my practice. Once you get up into your mid-80s, the doctors start calculating whether the treatments they can give you will prolong your life, or just prolong your suffering. For someone who's ninety, aggressive treatment would be cruel, almost."

"How could that be?" I said. "Old people want to keep living, too."

"Sure. But how much longer is the person likely to live? Let's say the treatment will give you an extra five years of life, on average. But at ninety, your odds of living another five years are pretty slim to begin with. Would you want to spend your last few years on earth constantly sick from chemo and radiation? Or would you rather skip the treatments and enjoy the rest of your life for as long as you can?"

"From what Zed was telling me, that's what the doctors were pushing on them," Randy said. "But Granny knows how much longer she has, and she knows how much she needs to get done before then. She'd rather be sick for a little while now and get over it."

I looked at him with narrowed eyes. "What do you mean, she knows how much longer she has?"

Randy glanced at me. "She's renewing in 2025."

"Renewing," I said slowly. "You mean…dying?"

He smiled oddly and rocked his head from side to side. "Kind of. Not really. You'll have to ask her to explain it."

I snorted. "If I ever see her again. I haven't seen either her or Zed since my mother's funeral. She keeps sending emissaries instead."

"Emissaries?" he said with a chuckle. "Like who?"

"Well, you, for one," I said. "And Janie at Cahokia."

"Oh, hey, I know Janie," he said with a grin. "She's good people."

"And Dirk the shaman," I said.

He laughed. "That guy? He only thinks he's a shaman."

I smiled to myself. "I sort of got that impression, yeah."

"Now I can introduce you to a *real* medicine man," he said. "But let's get you to Chaco first, so you can see what you need to see there."

His phrasing seemed odd, but I decided to let it go. We were on our way to the place where the thunderbirds wanted me to go. Maybe I'd learn more there.

The travel folks definitely were not kidding about the condition of the road to Chaco Canyon. It took us nearly an hour to cover the last several miles of washboard road.

"Why doesn't the state pave this?" Rick asked.

Randy smirked at him. "And let all the *bilagáana* tourists drive up here in their RVs and trash the place? No thanks." He spun the wheel to avoid a particularly large pothole, but we caught the edge of it anyway. "You're lucky you came in the summer," he went on cheerfully. "In the winter, this road ices over. Then it's impassable."

"It's not far from it now," Rick said, bracing himself with his right arm so he wouldn't slam into the door.

"Of course, summer can be bad, too," Randy said in the same chipper tone. "This road turns into a mudhole when it rains. Lucky for you folks, we haven't had any rain to speak of in weeks."

"Spectacular," Rick muttered, as we hit another pothole.

It was a relief when we reached pavement again. A few miles later, we entered the park.

"We'll stop first at the visitor center so you folks can get your bearings," Randy said. He continued speaking, but I stopped listening. All my attention was focused on a massive butte to our right.

"What is that?" I asked, pointing.

"Oh, that's Fajada Butte," Randy said. "You used to be able to hike up to the top, but the Park Service closed the trail back in the '80s. Too many people were going up there to see the Sun Dagger and the path eroded to the point where it was too dangerous."

I could hardly tear my eyes away from the butte. "What's the Sun Dagger?"

"What it *was*," he said, and paused. I turned my head and met his eyes. "What it *was* was a rock outcropping that allowed the ancestors who built this place to predict the solstices and equinoxes."

"Really?" I said. I flashed on a memory of an equinox ritual I'd conducted in my old life – back when I was a shaman for the tribe we now called the Hopewell. Back when my turtle and bird effigies were new.

Randy was watching me carefully – or as carefully as he could while not driving us off the road. "Really," he said. "They were even able to track the major and minor lunar standstills."

I caught my breath.

Either Randy didn't notice or decided not to. "The rangers at the visitor center can tell you more about it," he went on. "But there's no point in hiking up there now, even if you didn't break your neck on the path or get bitten by a rattlesnake."

"Why not?" I asked. I felt Rick stiffen next to me.

"Because it's broken," Randy said. "The dagger was focused by three big slabs of rock. But in 1989, the rocks shifted out of alignment. So they don't create a sun dagger any more."

"That's so sad," I said.

"Yeah, it is. It had only been rediscovered about ten years before that, and then it was gone."

Silently, I looked at the butte again. My Midwestern common sense was telling me to listen to Randy and the park rangers – all the people who knew better – and stay away from Fajada Butte. But my inner sense – the one that had guided me to the Great Circle, and to the RV I'd ended up buying, and to any number of other odd places and things over the course of the last few months – that inner sense was telling me I needed to go up to the top of that butte.

All I needed to do was find a way.

I glanced at Randy, and caught him eyeing me speculatively. He knew, I realized. He knew what I was planning to do. What I *had* to do. And I was pretty sure he could either lead me up there, or put me in touch with someone who could. The question was whether he'd do it – and whether Rick would stop me.

Randy had been right. The visitor center had a whole exhibit on the Sun Dagger, and the archaeologist in me was fascinated by the simplicity of the design.

The three sandstone slabs Randy had mentioned had stood upright, their long edges braced against a rock wall, with space between them that allowed shafts of light to appear on the wall at certain times of the year. The slabs were positioned in such a way that they created a shaded space between them and the wall. Someone had etched two spirals on the wall; the larger one had nine grooves between the center and the outside ring, with the second, much smaller one positioned on its left. At the summer solstice, a single dagger of light shone on the large spiral, appearing to bisect it. At the winter solstice, two daggers appeared, one on either side of the large spiral. And at the equinoxes, a large dagger of light appeared between the fourth and fifth rings of the large spiral, cutting that half of the spiral in half, while a smaller dagger bisected the small spiral.

The ancient Anasazi, who built Chaco Canyon starting around 850 A.D., weren't the only supposedly primitive people who kept track of the movements of the sun, moon and stars. The ancient Irish had created Newgrange, a passage tomb whose inner chamber was lit by the sunrise on only one day a year, the winter solstice. Stonehenge was thought to have some timekeeping properties, among other things. Back in North America, the Hopewell incorporated astronomical sightlines into the geometry of the Newark Earthworks, of which the Great Circle was a part. And the exhibit at Chaco made it clear there were other, similar orientation devices incorporated into the design of the community here – as well as elsewhere, by other peoples, throughout the Southwest.

But Chaco was special for another reason: It appeared to have been the northern terminus of a trade route that stretched more than a thousand miles south, all the way into the heart of Mexico.

All the way to the city where my son lived.

I glanced out the window of the visitor center. Something was calling me to the top of Fajada Butte, and I knew it wouldn't leave me alone until I got there.

Randy drove us around the ring road, stopping at the various sites of interest so we could hike down and investigate the ruins for ourselves. The Anasazi – the ancestors of today's Pueblo Indians – had built several types of structures, including the Great Houses at Chaco and the cliff dwellings at Mesa Verde in Colorado. But they all included a kiva – a circular underground room used for ceremonies, with an access point called a *sipapu* in the roof.

At another time, I would have been fascinated by the topic and anxious to learn as much as I could. But I was distracted. Hulking in the back of my mind was Fajada Butte, and what I might find if I could just get up there.

We stopped for lunch around noon – Randy had somehow thought far enough ahead to bring along a picnic lunch for the three of us – and as we ate, I mulled over ways to get him alone so I could ask him about making the trip to the butte. I was beginning to think Rick knew something was up – he had stuck to my side all day like a burr on a sock.

At last, he excused himself to find a restroom. As soon as he was out of earshot, I turned to Randy, my question half-formed on my lips.

"No," he said, before I could get the words out. "Absolutely not. I'm not going to be responsible for taking a crazy *bilagaána* lady up Fajada Butte. Even if Granny did send you."

"Then who would?" I asked. "Randy, I *have* to get up there to see the Sun Dagger. I can't explain why I feel so strongly about it, but I do."

"It's not even there any more," he said.

I stayed silent, but pleaded with my eyes.

He looked away, his mouth set in a line. Finally, he turned back to me. "I might know someone who could do it," he said. "I can introduce you to him as soon as we're done here."

"That would be fine," I said.

"What would be fine?" Rick asked, rejoining us.

Randy grinned. "Maggie was just reminding me that I'd promised to show you folks a real medicine man. If we leave soon, we could do that this afternoon." In a confidential tone, he added, "I'm not sure I'd chance taking you folks back to your RV this afternoon anyway. Those clouds over there look like rain."

"What clouds?" Rick said, scanning the clear sky.

"It's settled, then," said Randy. "We'll finish up here and head over to my place. You folks can stay the night with me and meet a real Navajo medicine man." He glanced at me. "And then we'll see where we stand."

"Sounds good," I said.

Rick eyed the two of us, but said nothing.

Chapter 12

I thought the road to Chaco Canyon was rough. The route to Randy's trailer was over no road at all. We followed ancient ruts up and over ridges to a manufactured home in the middle of nowhere. The setting was spectacular, surrounded by stratified rock in otherworldly formations, and yet prosaic: Sheets hung on a clothesline at one side of the house, and a propane tank sat on the other.

"I thought Navajos lived in hogans," Rick said. "That's what Tony Hillerman had his characters living in."

Randy nodded. "A lot of traditional folks still do. But the Legendary Lieutenant had a house with a garden, you'll recall. And Jim Chee lived in a trailer."

I'd read some of Hillerman's mysteries, all but a couple of which were set in this part of the world. It hadn't dawned on me to connect the two until Rick mentioned it. "So do you fancy yourself a solver of mysteries like Chee?" I asked Randy.

"Nope," he said. "And anyhow, Chee's trailer wasn't like this one. He had a regular mobile home. This one is a Katrina trailer." He hopped out of the truck and slammed the door behind him; we followed suit. "The government gave them to the Indians after they stopped off-gassing. Or at least we were told they'd stopped off-gassing. Might not be true. It wouldn't be the first time the government's ever lied to an Indian." He opened the door and gestured grandly. "Welcome to my humble home."

I went in first. The place looked reasonably tidy for the home of a bachelor. I wondered briefly what Tim's place looked like these days — whether it was the same tangle of dirty clothes and sports equipment as his room had been when he was a teenager, or whether he'd learned to tidy up after himself. Maybe Ana had civilized him.

I was seized suddenly with an overwhelming desire to see my son. I needed to confirm with my own eyes that he was okay. More than ever, after finding Emmy in that hovel in San Pedro, I was concerned about what I would find when I got to Mexico.

"We didn't pack an overnight bag," Rick said behind me, breaking into my reverie.

"Don't worry about it," Randy said. "You can borrow something to wear tonight. Here, let me get supper started. I bet you folks are famished. We did a lot of walking today."

"I'm not really that hungry," Rick said.

The two men looked hard at one another for a moment. "Well, I am," said Randy, and strode to the kitchen to begin fixing us something to eat.

Rick took a seat on a chair just inside the door, as if prepared to bolt. "So where's this medicine man you want us to meet?"

Randy pointed out the kitchen window. "He lives over that way." He flashed us a grin. "In a hogan. But he's coming here tonight."

Rick eyed him. "How'd you contact him? We've been with you the whole time."

"Spirits," Randy said, his expression serious. Then he winked.

I chuckled. Rick didn't.

The medicine man arrived just as we were sitting down to eat. Sani Tso was gray-haired, with the kind of leathery skin people develop when they've spent years working outdoors in the sun and wind. But he didn't seem that old to me. A little older than Rick and me, but not as old as Granny.

"Pleased to meet you, Mr. Tso," I said, holding out my hand.

He shook it readily enough. "You're the *bilagaána* with the artifacts," he said.

"I am. My name is Maggie Brandt."

"Nokomtha," he said, surprising me. That was what I'd asked my grandchildren to call me. It meant *grandmother* in Shawnee. He held out his hand. "May I see?"

I assumed he meant my turtle and bird, although how he could have known about them, I had no idea. I pulled my necklace over my head and put the effigies in his outstretched hand. He examined them, turning them over and nodding to himself. Then he gave them back. "Welcome," he said. "The Navajo have never been at war with the Shawnee."

"I'm not here to start one," I said. "I'm just here to get some answers."

"Have a seat, Sani," said Randy, as he brought a large pot from the kitchen to the table. "We've got lamb stew and fry bread."

"Where'd the lamb come from?" Sani asked as we all sat down.

"The grocery store in Gallup," said Randy. "Don't go starting trouble."

"I'm not starting anything," Sani said, and ladled himself a big bowl of soup from the pot.

The stew was delicious. So was the fry bread, although I didn't want to think about how many calories were in it. I consoled myself with the thought that I'd be burning off a lot of them on the ascent to the top of Fajada Butte.

"So what does a medicine man do?" asked Rick.

"Many things," said Sani.

"Don't let him fool you," said Randy. "He knows what medicine men do. He's read Tony Hillerman." I thought he might be teasing, but he didn't crack a smile.

Sani grunted and took another piece of fry bread.

Rick tried again. "I mean, what are we in for tonight? Is there some kind of ceremony or…"

Randy looked up from his food and stared mildly at him. Rick ducked his head and went back to eating.

After Randy cleared away the dinner things, we moved to the living room. Rick, Randy, and I sat, but Sani stayed on his feet. He looked first at me and said, "Nokomtha, you are on an important journey. I understand you believe that climbing Fajada Butte is the next step in that journey."

"That's what my spirits are telling me," I said.

"I knew it," Rick muttered. Louder, he said, "Don't do it, Maggie. You'd be breaking federal law, not to mention body parts. You heard what

Randy said – the path is too dangerous. The Park Service closed it for good reason."

"I know all that," I began.

"And there's nothing to see up there," he went on. "The rock slabs collapsed. The dagger's gone. You'd be going on a fool's errand."

"I know," I repeated.

"But you want to go anyway." He sounded disgusted.

"I don't have a choice. Rick, we've had this conversation." I pulled out the necklace again and let it hang freely; there was no need to conceal it here. "I told you before we left Lawrenceburg that sometimes these guys take over. This is one of those times."

He glared at me. "Well, I'm not going."

"No one expects you to," Randy said.

Rick's gaze snapped to the younger man.

Randy went on, "I'm not even going. Sani's going to take her. He knows the way." He pointed at the older man with his chin. "That's why he's here."

"Are you ready, Nokomtha?" Sani asked me.

"You mean now?" I squeaked.

"Now would be best," he said. "The moon will rise soon. We will need her light on the way back down."

I shrugged. "All right. I guess we might as well get it over with." I avoided looking at Rick. Instead, I said to Randy, "I didn't bring a jacket, though. I didn't realize we'd be gone so long."

In response, he reached behind the couch and pulled out a finely-woven throw that featured red and black stripes on a white background. "Wrap yourself up in it," he said.

I stood and shook out the throw, then slipped it around my shoulders. Randy smiled and nodded with appreciation.

"Okay, Sani," I said. "I guess we should get going. The night's not getting any younger."

Either Sani's truck's suspension was better than Randy's, or our guide had been showing off earlier, because the drive back to Chaco was much less bone-jarring with Sani behind the wheel. "Your friend – boyfriend?" he inquired.

"I guess so. We're not married."

He nodded. "Your boyfriend is not very supportive."

That made me laugh. "He's a lawyer. He believes it's his job to point out every flaw in my reasoning and every possible danger I could get into."

"Acknowledging danger is important. Avoiding it, if possible, is smart. But a person can be *too* careful."

"Yeah." I paused. "It feels like sometimes he looks for trouble unnecessarily."

"He's right about the danger here," Sani said. "But people have been making this sacred climb for thousands of years. The steps are worn, but not impassable. And when we get to the top, we will see what message the spirits have for us."

"Sounds good," I said.

Sani parked the truck in a pullout as close to Fajada Butte as he could get, and we walked the rest of the way. Before we began the climb, Sani pulled out a little bundle of sage and sweetgrass and lit one end, blowing on it until it began to smoke. Chanting softly, he waved the smoke over and around us. I didn't understand the words, but I assumed he was asking the spirits of this place to protect us and show me what I needed to see.

With the summer sunlight beginning to fade, we started up the four-hundred-eighty feet to the top.

The trail was steep and rutted, but maneuverable. The stairs, when we got to them, were less so. I was breathing hard by the time we got to the place where the Sun Dagger used to show itself. "Oh," I breathed in dismay. It was true. The three stone slabs had toppled over. There was no way to see anything here.

Sani began chanting again. He brushed past me and bade me follow him. And as I reached the entrance to the space behind the stones, my turtle began to glow.

As the medicine man kept up his chant, the turtle burned brighter and brighter, until it was blinding. Normally it gave off a copper-colored glow, but now the light was white-hot and dazzling.

As soon as I stepped into the niche, the show began.

The Sun Dagger appeared, making its paces through the year: first the autumn equinox, with the large and small daggers; then the winter solstice, with twin daggers on either side of the spiral; then the spring equinox, with the large and small daggers again; and finally the summer solstice, with the single dagger breaking the spiral in half. Then the dance began again. And again. Faster and faster, the daggers danced through the years, forming an intricate pattern I realized I'd seen before – on the back of my turtle.

The ancient Anasazi were no relation to the Hopewell, but they understood the importance – the sacred duty – involved in renewing the earth. Here atop Fajada Butte, the Sun Daggers had done the job for millennia. But time had taken its toll; the clockwork had eventually wound down. Now, I understood, the next renewal would be up to me.

I touched the spiral in thanks, and glanced outside. Then I gasped. For in the skies outside, another light show was playing – the moon was going though its paces, swinging back and forth across the sky between its positions at the major and minor standstills. And the moonlight delineated one more thing: An ancient Great Road that shot straight south from Chaco to a place I'd never heard of before.

"Teotihuacán," I whispered.

I didn't know where it was – only that I had a job to do there. Moreover, there was a bobble in the otherwise straight path – a place where I would find someone who needed my help in renewing themselves. Because that was my job, and had been since the days when the Great Circle was new. As Kokumthena had told me through Granny on the day this all began, *it is only by humanity's renewal that the Earth itself may be renewed.*

The Great Road faded from my sight; the moon took up its normal position in the sky. I returned to where Sani had been standing through it all. "Did you see it?" I asked.

He nodded. "Do you understand what you must do?"

"Yes." I looked south, where my destiny lay. "Yes, I do." I took a deep breath and in a more normal tone, I said, "Rick's not gonna like this one bit."

Chapter 13

Boy, was that ever an understatement.

On the return trip, Sani and I talked a little. But my head and heart were so full of what I'd seen that I barely knew what either of us was saying.

One thing, though, stuck with me. It was something Sani said: "Your boyfriend is on his own journey."

I knew that. I'd known it ever since Buddha Beach in Sedona. And it had nothing to do with the bucket-list itinerary he'd been so anxious to take me on before we left Lawrenceburg.

"So your paths may diverge for a little while," Sani went on.

I looked at him in surprise. "What? Now?" I said.

"Maybe now. Maybe not. But soon." He nodded, his eyes never leaving the road.

So I wasn't all that surprised at Rick's reaction when we got back to Randy's. When I walked in, Rick was sitting in the same uncomfortable posture in the chair closest to the door. He took one look at my face and his expression closed like a fist. Then he brushed past Sani and me and went out into the night.

"Coffee?" Randy asked quietly. "It may be a long night."

I waved him off and went after Rick.

He hadn't gotten far, and anyway he was easy to pick out, silhouetted as he was in the moonlight. He had to have heard me coming – I was physically tired from the climb up the butte, and I was dragging my feet more than walking. But he didn't turn to face me. Instead, he addressed the night. "You're going to Mexico," he said.

I stopped just behind him. "Of course. That's been the plan all along."

"That was *your* plan all along."

I was silent. He wasn't wrong.

At last, he turned to me. The moon lit his face unevenly, leaving half or more in shadow. "And I suppose you plan to drive all the way there."

"Rick," I began. "I saw the route from the top of the butte. It's a straight shot…"

"It's not," he said. "The magic or hallucination or whatever you experienced up there is making you think it's going to be a straight shot, but it's not. There are border guards in the way, and drug smugglers, and places where people get killed for no reason." His voice broke on the last words. "You heard what Emily said. She agreed with me. Why would you risk your life on such a foolhardy trip?"

What's the matter *with you, Maggie?* echoed in my head. Not in Rick's voice, though – in my brother Sandy's. In the voice of the man who had belittled me all the days of life, for nearly sixty years.

And in Gene's voice.

And in Ruth's voice.

And in my mother's voice.

And in the voice of my boss at the casino.

Anger flared in my chest.

In the corner of my brain that was still capable of rational thought, I knew I wasn't being fair to Rick. He was not Sandy – not by a long shot. He was simply being cautious. And I knew he spoke from a place of love.

But I'd lived on this earth for a long time, and I'd had enough of people telling me what an idiot I was.

"Why?" I said. "Because I have to."

"But…"

"And who are you to tell me how to live my life? I told you before we left Lawrenceburg that this trip wasn't a vacation. I have *work* to do. And I can't do it if I park the RV in Albuquerque and fly down to Mexico. If I fly, I will miss a crucial stop on my journey." Warmth spread out from my breastbone, but I ignored it. The effigies couldn't light me up any more than I already was.

He seemed to shrink before my onslaught. "I'm just worried about you, that's all. I want you to be careful."

"Sometimes," I said, remembering what Sani had said, "a person can be *too* careful."

He straightened, and his voice took on a wheedling tone. "Look, Maggie May. I understand that you feel that you need to drive down to Mexico City. But that RV…" He chuckled. "You know it's already broken down on us twice. We've been lucky so far – we've always been in hailing distance of a mechanic who could fix it. But how do you know our luck will hold south of the border?"

"I don't," I said.

"What if it breaks down in the middle of the desert? How are you going to find someone to fix it? Do you speak Spanish?"

"You know I don't," I said.

"Do you think the drug lords' paramilitary troops speak English?"

I threw up a hand between us. "Just stop," I said. "You've made your point."

"Good."

"And I'm still taking the RV to Mexico City."

We stood there in the moonlight for another few moments, arms locked against each other. I had a fleeting thought of what a normal couple would be doing in the moonlight, and closed my eyes. Nothing ever seemed easy for me.

"Let's call Tim," Rick said.

My eyes flew open. "Now?"

"Of course not," he scoffed. "There's no signal out here. No, when we get back to Gallup tomorrow. Let's call him and see what he says about this…idea of yours."

He had very nearly said it was a *crazy* idea. That unspoken word hung in the air between us.

I had a choice: I could make an issue of it now, or skip it. Was it worth renewing the fight? He'd managed to stop himself in time – I had to give him credit for that.

Maybe I should have challenged him. But it was late, and I was tired and getting cold; the temperature seemed to be in free-fall. "Fine," I said at last. "When we get back to Gallup, I'll call Tim."

"Fine," he said.

Randy lent us t-shirts to sleep in, and his spare bedroom. The mattress sagged in the middle – no matter what we did, we could not stay on opposite sides of the bed.

It was a very uncomfortable night.

I got up as soon as there was a glimmer of light in the sky, dressed as quietly as I could, and left Rick snoring softly. I'd expected to be the first one up, but Randy had beaten me to it. Coffee was brewing in the coffee maker on the counter.

I stepped to the kitchen window and glimpsed our host standing barefoot in the cold dirt, facing the rising sun. He held out his hand and let a pinch of yellow powder blow away on the dawn wind.

I scurried away and took a seat at the dinette.

A few minutes later, Randy came in. He gave me a surprised smile. "*Yá'át'ééh abíní*," he said. "Good morning, Maggie. The coffee's almost ready."

"I know," I said. "Good morning to you, too."

"Is Rick up yet?"

"Nope."

"That's a stroke of luck." Randy sat across from me at the table. "I wanted to talk to you about this idea of yours."

"Sani told you while we were outside arguing, didn't he?" I said.

"He didn't have to. I heard Rick say, 'Mexico,' and figured it out on my own," he said. "Doesn't he understand the necessity behind a sacred journey?"

"Sacred journey," I said with a lopsided grin. "I like the sound of that. It's better than 'crazy woman is trying to get herself killed.'"

"He thinks it's inevitable," he said.

"Let's just say the probability is higher than he's comfortable with. But he's willing to let my son Tim make the final decision." I explained quickly that Tim would have a better sense of the situation in Mexico, as he lived there.

"That seems fair," Randy said. "But Maggie – you should not let anyone else make the decision for you. Take their counsel, yes. Weigh your options, yes. But Granny has expectations for each of us, and fulfilling those expectations has to be paramount."

"Of course, you're right. Like I told Rick last night, I have a job to do. Just because it's dangerous or inconvenient doesn't mean I can get out of doing it."

"Oh, you can try to get out of it," he said. "But Kokumthena has a knack for making your life difficult until you do what she wants you to do." He glanced over his shoulder at the same time the coffee maker gave out its final gasp. "Coffee's ready. Cream? Sugar?"

"Just cream, thank you. I can get my own."

He was already out of his chair. "It's no trouble," he said, and grabbed a couple of mugs from an upper cabinet.

"Randy?" I said as he poured. "You're Navajo, right?"

"Right."

"So why are you doing the bidding of a Shawnee spirit? Why aren't you following your own gods?"

He put a full mug down in front of me. "Who says I'm not?"

Rick rose shortly thereafter. I took a mug of coffee to our room for him as a peace offering. In return, he smiled and kissed me. I think he believed he was going to win.

Not long after, we hit the road again in Randy's truck. Our host and guide kept up a steady patter, pointing out the local landmarks and telling us stories about them – none of which, unfortunately, I retained. Rick, though, was cordial, and asked about some of the scenes from Tony Hillerman's novels.

I half believed we'd get back to the RV and find it vandalized – spray-painted with gang symbols, maybe, or up on blocks with all four tires gone. But it was still parked in the diner's lot where we'd left it the day before.

"I'm starving," I announced before Randy drove off. "Let's get something to eat, shall we?" I turned to our guide. "It's on us. It's the least we can do for the hospitality you've shown us."

"I never turn down free food," he said with a grin.

Inside, the same waitress brought us coffee and menus. "How was your trip?" she asked. "Did you get up to Chaco?"

"We did," I said, "and it was unforgettable." I avoided looking at Rick.

As soon as she was out of earshot, Rick said, "See if you've got a signal on your phone."

Four of five bars were lit. "I do," I said. "But let's eat before we call. I don't want to do this on an empty stomach."

I went for the breakfast burrito, Christmas style. Rick had chorizo with his scrambled eggs, and Randy went for Spam with his eggs. "It's an acquired taste," he said as he dug in.

"So I've heard," I said, amused. "I've never acquired it."

Rick ignored us.

I ate slowly, stalling for as long as I could, but eventually I'd downed every last bite of my burrito. I put my napkin on the table and looked up at my companions. "It was good," I said. "Very tasty."

"It was," said Rick brusquely. "But we need to get going."

I picked up my phone from the table, and hesitated. "Let's adjourn to the RV," I said. "We'll have more privacy there." And I led Randy across the parking lot to the rig, leaving Rick to pay the bill and catch up to us.

Once inside, Randy squeezed in on one side of the dinette table and Rick took the opposite bench, so that they were facing each other. It almost felt like I was being asked to take sides – so I stood. I placed my phone on the table, called Tim, and turned on the speaker so everyone could hear it.

"*Dígame,*" my son said. "Oh, hi, Mom. I didn't see the number at first."

"That's okay. Hi, sweetie. Can you hear me okay? I put the phone on speaker because I have a couple of people here with me."

"Sure, you're loud and clear. Hi, everybody." I could just imagine him waving to these people he couldn't see."

"Hi, Tim, it's Rick Hughes," he said. "I don't think we've met."

"Oh, hey, Rick. My sisters and Riley told me about you."

"I hope it was all good," I said with a smile.

"Yeah, it was. I'm looking forward to meeting him."

"That's kind of what I'm calling about," I said. "But there's one other person here."

Randy spoke up. "Randy Daschine," he said in his high tenor. "I'm a friend of Granny's."

"Nice to virtually meet you," Tim said. "You're bringing quite a crowd, Mom. When are you arriving?"

"That's what we wanted to talk to you about," I said.

Rick broke in. "Your mother wants to drive her RV across the border. All the way to Mexico City."

Tim was silent for a moment. Then he said, "Oh."

Rick raised his arms and looked significantly at me. I wasn't going to cede so easily, though. "What do you mean by that?" I asked my son.

"Well," he said, and paused. "It's just that things are a little rough in much of the country right now. Crime-wise."

"That's what I've been trying to tell her," Rick said, hunching forward with his forearms resting on the table. "I think it's a bad idea to drive. And not just because of the drug lords. We've had a couple of breakdowns with this rig already. There's no telling what might happen if it broke down again, in a foreign country. And neither your mother nor I speak Spanish." He straightened and sat back. The phrase, *The prosecution rests, Your Honor*, floated through my mind.

"I do," Randy said.

Rick's eyebrows shot up and his chin came down. "You speak Spanish?"

"Yeah."

Rick was still dubious. "Are you saying you're willing to make the trek with us?"

Randy shrugged. "Why not? I'm between jobs right now." He said this as if it were an inside joke. I suspected being between jobs was pretty much constant for him. "And I have marching orders from Granny, too."

"Mom?" Tim said. "What's he talking about?"

I filled him in on the message I'd received at the Sun Dagger site. "So I know I'm supposed to go to Teotihuacán," I said, "and I can't fly because there's an interim stop I need to make."

"Where?"

"I don't know yet. I assume I'll know it when I get there. That's how it's always worked up to now."

"You see how crazy this is?" Rick said to Tim. "Your mother agreed that she would let you decide whether it was safe for her to drive."

"What I said, Rick," I broke in, "was that I would hear Tim's opinion. The final decision still lies with me."

"That's not what we agreed to," he said.

"We didn't agree to anything except that I would call Tim," I shot back.

"Whoa, whoa, whoa," said Randy with a chuckle. "If you two don't stop bickering, you'll never find out what he thinks."

Rick and I locked gazes for a moment. Then I tried a disarming grin. "He's right," I said. "Sorry, Rick."

"I'm sorry, too," he said, but he wasn't smiling. He turned again to the phone. "So Tim, what's your verdict?"

"He's not…" I began.

"Mom, it's okay," Tim said, and paused. "Look. I can't make this decision for anybody – even you, Mom."

"That's okay," I said.

"What I can tell you is that it's safe enough where I am, in Mexico City – which is to say that it's about on a par with every other big city I've ever been in. And the neighborhood around Teotihuacán is fine. The problem will be getting here. Where are you planning to cross the border?"

I'd never gotten that far in my planning. "We're in Gallup, New Mexico, right now. If I were going in more or less a straight line from here, where would I cross?"

"El Paso, I think. But that brings you right into Chihuahua State. And then Durango and Zacatecas."

"Are those good?" I asked, though my heart was sinking.

"Not so much." His tone brightened. "But once you get to Guanajuato, you shouldn't have anything to worry about."

"How long is the drive?" Rick asked.

"From El Paso?" He paused. "Twenty, twenty-one hours, maybe."

"And how much of that is through dangerous territory? Chihuahua and Durango and the others?"

"Most of it," Tim admitted. "But if you stick to the *cuatos* – the toll roads – you'll be fine."

Rick sat back and crossed his arms. "You'd have to stop somewhere," he said.

"Not if we switch drivers," I said, "the way we did on the way to California."

"You want to drive after *dark*?" Rick said.

"If you stick to the *cuatos*..." Tim repeated.

"You're not helping," Rick growled.

"Not from your point of view, no," Tim said. "I know what you're after. You want me to talk Mom out of doing this."

Rick glowered at me but said nothing.

"And I'm not going to do that," Tim went on.

"Why?" Rick exploded. "For the love of all that's holy, *why*?"

"You just said why," Randy said. "It's for the love of all that's holy." He leaned forward. "Tim gets it, and I get it, and Maggie gets it, for sure. She's on a sacred journey, and sacred journeys are not always safe. But they are *always* necessary."

"So I'm just her bodyguard," Rick said bitterly.

"Don't be ridiculous," I said. "You matter to me. I wanted you to come, didn't I?"

He looked away.

"And it's not like Mom can't protect herself," Tim said. "She has some pretty powerful spirits backing her up."

I had a brief vision of Thunderbird lighting up a posse belonging to some drug lord, and shook my head to clear it. I hoped never to live through that experience again.

I glanced at Rick, and found him watching me closely. He looked slightly more mollified than he had a few minutes ago. He'd seen my effigies in action, after all. I began to wish he had come with Sani and me to see the Sun Dagger. Maybe then he'd understand the forces I was dealing with.

"How soon can we expect you?" Tim asked.

I drew in a breath. "It's, what, a day or so from here to El Paso? I think we'll stay the night there tonight, and then cross the border early tomorrow morning."

"The lines may be shorter early in the day," Randy said. "Got your passport?"

"Of course," I said. "Rick?"

"Yeah," he muttered.

"Mom, make sure you buy Mexican insurance for the RV," Tim said. "You can do that at the border. And call your cell phone provider and get them to put international roaming on your line."

"I never would have thought of that," I said. "Thank you, Tim."

"So we'll see you bright and early, the day after tomorrow," Tim said. "I can't wait to tell Ana. She's been so excited about meeting you."

"I can't wait to meet her, either," I said. "See you soon, sweetie." I ended the call, and turned to Randy. "You're really coming with us?"

"Zed told me Granny said I need to," he said. "I'm not about to cross her."

Chapter 14

Rick had slept better than I had, so he drove us to Albuquerque. I crawled up into our bed over the cab and tried to sleep with my clothes on. I was mostly unsuccessful, but I must have dozed off for a little while, because I remembered dreaming about spiders. The petroglyphs had come to life and were web-swinging their way south, dragging me, bound in silver strands, along behind them.

I came awake with a start, and realized the RV had stopped moving. There was no sound from below, either. I climbed down from the bed and peered out, assuming we'd stopped for gas, or maybe lunch. But we were parked at a curb beside a long building. The sign over one door said, "Departures."

I slipped my shoes on and stepped out the door onto the sidewalk. Randy stood some distance away, arms crossed, with an inscrutable expression on his face. He nodded to me. I started toward him, but he called, "Stay with the RV. In case we have to move it."

I retreated to the passenger side door. "Where's Rick?" I called.

"He'll be along."

A few moments later, Rick walked through the glass doors. He checked his stride when he saw me, but kept on coming.

I willed time to stop, or at least to rewind. But the spirits helping me knew how to turn time in only one direction.

"You're not coming," I said when he reached me.

"I can't," he said. "I can't watch you do this. I think it's wrong and dangerous and I…" He swallowed. "I wouldn't be any good to you. I can't stop you and I can't save you. I can't even say the right thing anymore." He chuckled bitterly. "Some counselor I've turned out to be."

"You're more than my counselor," I said, placing a hand on his shoulder. "You're my best friend." I blinked back tears. "Please come with me. It won't be the same without you."

He shook his head.

"Then meet me in Mexico City. Please, Rick. I know you don't want to make the drive, but come and be with me there."

He closed his eyes. "Maybe. I need to think about it."

I dropped my hand. He caught it in his. "What are you going to do?" I asked.

"I don't know. I bought a ticket to Cincinnati." He sucked in a breath. "Bright and early tomorrow morning. I'll be back home by lunch time."

"Is that what you want to do? Go home?"

"I don't know," he said. "No. I do know." His gaze was anguished. "I want to be with you."

"Then…"

"But not like this." He waved at the RV. "Will you come home to me? When this is all over, will you come home?"

I shook my head, remembering the *thud* of an unseen door closing as I had crossed the Kentucky state line. "Indiana's not my home any more."

He nodded and stared at the sidewalk. "I think I knew that." He looked up. "Well. You should get going. I can get a taxi to a hotel from here."

"I love you," I said, knowing it was probably the worst possible thing to say.

"I love you, too, Maggie May." He wrapped his arms around me and held me for what seemed like forever. Then he walked away.

An unseen door clanged shut in my head.

I don't know how I held myself upright. It *couldn't* be over, I thought. This was another bad dream, like the spider silk, or like the water panther lying in wait for a disoriented doe. I'd awaken in just a moment and roll over, and Rick would be next to me in bed and everything would be all right again.

Randy stepped up next to me and opened the passenger door. "Get in," he said kindly. "I'll drive."

For the rest of the day, I went through the motions of living – eating, drinking water, responding to Randy's questions – but I was wasn't really there. Randy, bless him, understood. He drove all the way to El Paso. He even picked an RV park without consulting me. Then he parked the rig and set the leveling jacks by himself – while I sat inside and stared at nothing.

When he came back in, he said, "There's a restaurant across the road. The guy parked next to us says the food is pretty good. Do you want to go over there or make something here?"

"I don't care," I said. Then I remembered that with Rick gone, we were down to just my money. "But eating here would be cheaper."

"This place won't break the bank," he said. "Come on. I could use a walk after all that driving – and so could you."

I sighed and picked up my purse. "I guess."

Even as late in the day as it was, it was a hot and dusty walk. And the road we had to cross proved to be a two-lane highway with no stoplight. We waited for a break in the traffic and dashed across.

I felt a little more human after that derring-do, and even more when we entered the restaurant. It appeared to be an authentic hole-in-the-wall Mexican place, with signs in both Spanish and English. The TV above the bar was showing a bullfight, silently, with closed-captioning in Spanish.

"Does Mexico still allow bullfighting?" I asked our server.

"Yes, but some states do so no longer," he said, his English thickly accented. "Many people would like to see the bullfight banned. Many people think it is cruel to the bull. But it is a part of our culture."

I glanced at the TV, where someone was shoving a spear into the poor bull's neck, and looked away. "I think I agree with the people who think it's cruel."

"Want to see a bullfight while we're there?" Randy asked mischievously.

Our server smiled. "Do not worry, señora. It won't be possible. The bullfight is a winter sport."

"I'm relieved to hear it," I said.

After we ordered – Randy took the lead on that, too, bless him – he asked, "How did you get mixed up with Granny and Zed? You've never told me."

So I explained over dinner how I'd been led, almost, to the Great Circle Earthworks in Ohio, and had a spontaneous past-life regression while inside the circle. I'd been there before, in another body and another life, to receive my turtle effigy. I pulled my necklace out from under my t-shirt as I talked. "These were both mine in that other life. I found them both in nearly the same spot in a wooded area where I grew up, but decades apart. I found the turtle when I was a little girl, but the bird came back to me just a few months ago."

He looked, but didn't touch. "I can feel them from here. You must have been a powerful medicine woman."

"I think I was," I said, in a confiding tone. Then I cocked my head. "I've been saying I was a shaman. Should I be saying medicine woman? Is that more correct?"

"I don't think it matters," he said with a grin. "It's not like the Hopewell are around to tell you which is right."

"True," I said. "But see here? The design on the turtle's shell?" I traced part of it with a fingernail. "I had a vision not long ago that explained how this part of the design is a map of my life – of the way I should be walking. Or the way I should have been walking all along, really. But I was pushed off the path by ... circumstances. I've spent the last nine months or so trying to get back on the path." I dropped the effigies but didn't put them back in their hiding place. "I thought Rick was part of the solution. He was a big help to me in straightening out my mother's affairs before she died, and then again after she and my brother were killed in the fire. But now..." I looked away.

"Now you think he might have been part of the problem."

I shrugged. "Kind of, yeah. It just started to seem like everything he was advising me to do was wrong. He thought we should buy a bigger RV.

He wanted to see a lot more of the country, when I told him my main goals were to see Emily and Tim." I glanced at him. "Emily is my middle daughter. She lives in California."

"I picked that up, yeah," he said.

I nodded. "Anyway, then he didn't want me to go up Fajada Butte, when I knew I needed to do it. And you saw what he was like when I refused to fly to Mexico City. I've never thought of him as controlling, but maybe I've been wrong all these years."

"Years?" he asked. "How long have you guys known each other?"

"Since we were kids."

"And he didn't try to control you before," he said.

I laughed shortly. "If he'd been the controlling type back then, he wouldn't have let me marry Gene."

"That's your ex?"

"Yeah. Sorry. I know it's a lot to keep track of."

"I'm keeping up pretty well so far." He grinned, then leaned back as our meals arrived. Our combination plates were huge – two tacos, a tostada, refried beans, and rice. He picked up a taco, took a bite, and chewed with a beatific look on his face. "Ah, now we're talking," he said when he'd swallowed. "This is *real* Mexican food. None of your silly *americano* cuisine." He gestured toward my plate. "Go on, try it."

I bit into my taco. The ground meat inside was spiced, but not to the point that I needed to grab my water glass. And nothing on my plate was smothered in cheese. "This is really good," I said.

"Just like Mamecita used to make," he said, and wolfed down the rest of his taco. "So anyway," he said, moving on to the refried beans, "I'd say there's a difference between trying to control another person and wanting to keep them safe. I didn't get a controlling vibe from him. I think he just doesn't have all the information, and was talking from a position of prudence. At least about driving to Mexico," he added. "I can't speak to the rest of it, since I wasn't there."

"You don't think…"

He paused in mid-bite. "I think he's genuinely frightened for you."

I pondered that while I finished my taco. "Sani told me Rick was on his own journey," I said.

"We all are," Randy said. He looked up at me. "You mean now? Maybe. Maybe the split was necessary in the grand plan. He probably needs to catch up with you."

"Maybe," I conceded, and started on my second taco. "What about you?"

"Me?"

"Where are you in the grand plan? Were you a medicine man in a past life?"

He laughed. "If I was, Sani Tso would be very surprised."

"How did you meet Granny, then?"

"Oh, well, you know. In the usual course of things."

"Come on," I wheedled. "I told you my story. You owe me."

He eyed me speculatively. "All right," he said at last, and laid down his fork. "I was at Canyon de Chelly. You've heard of it?"

"I think so," I said doubtfully.

"The last word is spelled C-H-E-L-L-Y. Ring any bells now?"

"Oh!" He'd pronounced it *shay*. "Now I know what you're talking about. Yes, of course. We thought about stopping there. Isn't there a spire called Spider Rock?" As soon as I said it, my dream of being kidnapped by petroglyphs came back to me, and I shivered. My turtle bounced a little on my chest.

"Whoa," Randy said, watching it with widened eyes. "Did you do that, or did it do it on its own?"

"She did it herself," I said. "Go on."

"Hang on a sec. Lost my train of thought." He looked away for a moment. "Okay. Yes, Spider Rock is there – but it's actually two sandstone spires side by side. The taller one is the home of Spider Woman, Na'ashjéii Asdzáá.

"The Hopi consider her a creation spirit, but in our myths, she's more along the lines of a teacher of culture and survival. She taught us loom weaving and farming. And she's been known to rescue Diné boys in danger by dropping her web down the side of the spire and hauling them up to safety. But she's not a spirit to take lightly. Our parents used to warn us that if we misbehaved, Spider Woman would come and take us with her to her home. Supposedly the top of the spire was covered in the bones of wayward children." He smiled. "Of course, now that you can see the plateau from a plane, you learn pretty quick that it's not true. But the threat still works on the littlest ones."

I'd seen where the tale veered off-track. "Were you in danger?" I asked quietly.

"More or less." He glanced at the bar. "See all that liquor? I don't dare have any of it."

"You're an alcoholic."

He nodded. "Lots of us are. Most of the people live in poverty. Jobs are hard to come by. You've gotta do something to kill time." He glanced toward the bar again, then focused on me. "The day I ran into Granny and Zed, I was feeling as hopeless as anyone ever has, I guess. I knew the booze would kill me eventually, and I figured I'd beat it to the punch. So I decided to climb the shorter spire and throw myself off of it."

This was starting to sound familiar. Maybe a little too familiar. "Did Spider Woman drop a silken rope for you?"

"In a manner of speaking." He leaned forward and spoke so quietly that I could barely hear him over the noise of the bar. "I've never told anyone but Sani about this."

"My lips are sealed," I said.

"I know. That's why I'm telling you." He paused. "Anyway, I'd planned to do it fast and get it over with. Drive out, scurry up the thing, and jump before I lost my nerve. But on the day I had picked to do it, my departure kept getting delayed. I was really mad about it, because I knew it was getting to be too late to start the climb. So I brought some camping gear and built a fire at the base of the spire. I figured I'd sleep there and do the climb first thing in the morning." He snorted. "Then I got drunk and passed out. Usually I wouldn't remember anything when I'd come to, but this time was different. This time, I'd dreamed. And in my dream, Spider Woman had caught me up with a strand of her silk and pulled me up to her house. She fed me a kind of stew and told me it would heal me of the craving for alcohol.

"I asked her why she was helping me, and she said she needed *my* help. She said it was on behalf of a sister goddess."

"Kokumthena?" I asked.

"That's what I figured after I met Granny." He sat back. "Which happened really fast. When I woke up that morning, the two of them were walking across the canyon floor toward me. Now, you need to understand that Canyon de Chelly is Navajo land. Tribal land. It's part of the reservation – the National Park Service helps us run it, but the park is ours and the land is sacred. We don't let any *bilagaána* wander around by themselves. They have to have an escort. So here come Granny and Zed, stumbling across my campsite, right? I jump up out of my sleeping bag and demand to know what they're doing there. And Granny sits down on the ground and speaks to me, and the breeze she brings is *green*." He shook his head in wonder at the memory. "Green like a forest, maybe. Like it had just rained."

"That's Kokumthena, all right," I said. "What did she tell you? Did she say anything about doors closing?"

He looked baffled. "No, nothing like that. Just that I'd be contacted by a woman who wanted to see the Sun Dagger, and that whatever she needed done, I needed to help her do it."

My eyes widened. "Oh," I said. "Well, that explains how you knew Granny had sent me."

"Yep."

"When was this?"

He shrugged. "A year ago, maybe. I've seen them once since then, and Zed a couple of times after Granny got sick. So like I said, I had a pretty good idea of when you were going to show up."

"Why you, though?" I blurted.

He spread his hands wide. "I have no idea. And Granny wouldn't tell me. I asked her."

"What about Spider Woman? Did you ask *her*?"

"She has not manifested to me since. But her cure worked. I haven't touched alcohol since that night, and I don't feel a desire for it, either. But even so, I stay as far away from temptation as I can." He cast a wary eye toward the bar.

"Good for you," I said automatically. "So I guess Kokumthena is the sister goddess she was talking about."

"I don't think so," he said. "She pointed south when she said it. When you guys started arguing about Mexico, I thought maybe it was you."

"Me?" I said, shocked. "I'm no goddess!"

He glanced at my effigies. "I wouldn't be too sure about that."

We defied danger again shortly thereafter by running back across the highway to the RV park – although in my case, it was more of a waddle.

"Let's get some shut-eye," Randy said. "I'd like to get up before the sun, and try to beat the crowd through the border crossing."

"Okay," I said. I felt wrung out myself. I slipped up into the bed over the cab; Randy folded out the couch and made himself comfortable. It wasn't long before I heard him breathing deeply in slumber.

I wished I'd been able to drift off as easily. I missed Rick. We hadn't been together all that long – not as significant others, anyway – but I'd gotten used to having him next to me, both figuratively and literally.

His pillow was still here, and it smelled like him. I hugged it and shed a few silent tears, and eventually I fell asleep.

Chapter 15

Even as early as we got there, the line to cross the border was long. The guards seemed bored. They asked us a number of questions, examined our passports, and directed us to the place where we could buy Mexican insurance for the RV. The rates were astronomical, but I paid. There didn't seem to be much choice.

We also picked up some printed information about recent criminal activity and safety advice. As Tim had said, as long as we stuck to the *cuotas*, it looked like we'd be fine.

The whole process took several hours. "Good thing we started early," I said once we'd run the gantlet, "or we'd be looking for a place to have supper right about now."

"No kidding," Randy said, tossing me the keys. "You drive. See how far we can get before you need a break. I'm planning to do the driving when it's dark out."

"Why?"

"If we get stopped at night, I'd rather it looked like I was alone."

"I guess that makes sense," I said, and got in the driver's seat.

The scenery here, across the Rio Grande, was very like the parts of Texas and New Mexico we'd been driving through for the past few days — lots of scrubby plants, cacti, and reddish dirt. I shouldn't have been surprised. Desert is desert, no matter what language the highway signs are in.

The pavement wasn't the smoothest I've ever driven on, but it was okay. Better than the Navajo reservation's "roads," although I wasn't about to tell Randy that.

Some distance south of Ciudad Juarez, we were waved over at one official-looking checkpoint. I rolled down the window and did my best to look bewildered at the rapid-fire Spanish the guard barked at me. Then I handed him all of the paperwork we'd received when we bought our insurance at the border, and pointed mutely to the sticker on the windshield. He fanned through the papers briefly, nodded, and handed them back. Then he waved me on.

"*Gracias*," I managed as I accelerated slowly. It wasn't until we were well clear of the checkpoint that I realized my hands were trembling. I began to wonder whether I should have listened to Rick, after all.

But no – I had a job to do somewhere south of Chihuahua. And the closer we got, the more certain I was that it needed to be done.

Around lunchtime, Randy put together some sandwiches and handed me one, together with a can of pop. I put the can in a cup holder and popped the top with one hand. Then I took a bite from the sandwich – turkey lunchmeat with mayo. "Thanks."

"Want to switch off?" he asked.

"No, I'm fine. You can take a nap if you want."

"I will, after I eat." And he took a seat at the dinette and polished off two sandwiches in record time. I watched him via the rear-view mirror.

When I allowed myself to think about the situation I was in, I became mildly alarmed. Here I was, in a foreign country where I didn't speak the language, driving an unwieldy vehicle with a tendency to break down – and my sidekick was a guy I'd met only a couple of days before. All I knew about him was that he'd been a drunk – and I was taking him at his word that he wasn't a drunk any more – and that Granny and Zed vouched for him, albeit second- or third-hand. Moreover, my only connection to home had bailed on me. And – here I picked up my phone – I had no cell signal. I knew the service worked in Mexico – I'd received a text from the Mexican phone network shortly after we crossed the border – so that wasn't the problem. The problem was there was no coverage here, and there probably wouldn't be until we got closer to a city.

On the other hand, I thought as I glanced again in the rear-view mirror, Randy hadn't done anything suspicious or untoward so far. He hadn't raised a hand to me, hadn't made a pass at me, and seemed to consider me a friend – or at least someone who deserved respect. Whether he respected me personally or my effigies, I wasn't entirely sure, and it probably didn't matter for the purposes of this trip.

We made it to Chihuahua around two in the afternoon. Randy seemed refreshed after his midday nap, so we switched off for a few hours. When I'd consulted Google Maps in El Paso, it said it was about six hours from Chihuahua to Torreón, and another five and a half hours from there to Aguascalientes. It was a further six hours from Aguascalientes to Mexico City, but the good news was that we would be in friendly territory then. Or at least not actively hostile territory.

If all went well, we'd be in Mexico City just in time for morning rush hour.

We swapped drivers again near Torreón, with a brief stop for gas and some food. As I got back in the driver's seat, I felt a warmth at my breastbone. That, plus my internal homing instinct, told me we were nearing the point I'd been both anticipating and dreading since I'd climbed Fajada Butte. I swallowed and started the rig.

The sun was heading toward the western horizon when I saw a bunch of people standing in the road in front of us. As I got closer, I could see they were dressed in desert camouflage and carried nasty-looking rifles. "Randy," I said quietly.

In an instant, he came forward from the couch and leaned over the console, one elbow braced on the back of my seat. "I'll talk to them," he said. "You just do what they tell you to do."

"This is it," I said.

"I know."

One of the men held up his hand, and I slowed the vehicle to a stop, my heart beating wildly. My turtle rattled against my bird. The racket sounded like castanets. I put my hand to my throat to stop them.

Randy got in the passenger seat and rolled down the window. He and the man who had stopped us had a short conversation; Randy tried to hand over the paperwork we'd gotten at the border, but the man waved him off.

I saw all that, but my attention was focused elsewhere: on the knot of quasi-soldiers at the side of the road. There were four of them, all dressed in camo, all armed like the man Randy was talking with. Three of them were watching me and sniggering. The fourth stared at me as if I were his salvation.

He was the one I was supposed to help. But how? I didn't speak Spanish, and his buddies looked like they'd just as soon hurt me as allow me to help him.

"Maggie," Randy said. I dragged my gaze away from the men I'd been watching. "He wants us to get out of the car."

"Okay," I said, and opened the door. Randy got out on the other side, and we stepped to the side of the road together.

The captain, for so he seemed to be, reeled off an order in gruff Spanish. The leering trio straightened and made for the back door of the RV. "Inspection, señora," the captain said with a wicked smile.

I nodded brusquely.

My quarry was in front of his compatriots, but his steps lagged. One of the leering men called to the captain, who barked at the guy in front. The tattler then jabbed my guy in the small of his back with the butt of his gun, nearly sending him sprawling.

"Hey!" I yelled. "Leave him alone!"

"Maggie," Randy said. "I don't think this is a good time."

Tattler left his buddies and slouched toward me. I could read his intention in his eyes. He reached one hand up as if to caress my cheek, but I knew he planned more. My bird blazed forth its golden light as my arm came up to block him. He yelled in pain and cradled his arm while cringing away from the light.

The man I was here to help shouted what sounded like a name. The others rounded on him and began beating him with their firearms.

Randy grabbed the gun away from the man I'd hurt and fired a round into the sky, which got everyone's attention. Training the gun on the fake troops, he shouted at them. I assume he told them to drop their weapons and raise their hands, because that's what they did. Next, Randy spoke for a few moments, gesturing at me and at my effigies. He pointed south, still talking. Then he addressed the captain with a question. Reluctantly, the captain answered. Randy said something else, brandishing the gun as if telling them to move out.

The man I'd injured shot a glare at me, and then joined his compatriots. Two of his leering friends grabbed the man they'd been beating by his arms and hoisted him to his feet.

"Let him go," I said. "He's coming with us."

Randy translated. The boy turned toward us, astonished. How had I not noticed before that he was still a boy? He couldn't have been more than eleven or twelve. I beckoned to him; he glanced around at the men, and ran to my side.

I gave him a smile, which he returned tentatively.

"Grab the guns," Randy said to me. I walked forward to pick up the firearms and bundled them awkwardly in my arms. I hoped I didn't shoot anyone accidentally.

"Get in the RV," Randy said. "Now."

I was never so happy to comply to an order. Our guest scurried after me and climbed in; I heard his breath catch as he saw the interior of the RV. I turned around and grinned at him. Then I started the engine.

Randy jumped in and said, "Go." I never would have thought it possible to squeal the tires on an RV, but I managed it.

The two of us exchanged a glance and simultaneously breathed a big sigh of relief. Then Randy turned to our guest, who was still regarding us with wide eyes. He must have asked the boy his name, because he replied, "Carlito Martinez."

"*Buenos días*, Carlito," I said, in my horrible Spanish accent.

"*Buenos días, diosa*," he said politely.

"What's *diosa?*" I asked Randy.

He smirked at me. "He thinks you're a goddess."

"Oh, no. Not him, too." I rolled my eyes. "Tell him I'm not."

He looked at me mischievously. I glared back at him. "Oh, all right," he said, and turned back to the boy. The conversation that followed ended with Carlito looking unconvinced.

I gave up and moved on. "How old is he? Where's he from? Can we take him home?"

Randy nodded along with my questions, and then turned back to our charge. Never have I wanted more to speak and understand another language than I did at that moment.

"He says he's from Parras, in Coahuila State. His parents are dead, killed in the crossfire when a drug deal went bad. His only surviving sibling is the guy who whacked him with his rifle back there."

"That was his brother?" I said, horrified.

Randy nodded. "That's what he told me. He went to Chihuahua after his parents died to live with his brother, but discovered he'd been dragged into this drug lord's security detail."

"And he got swept up into it himself," I said.

"That's what he says."

"Any other family?"

"An aunt in Mexico City."

"How fortunate that we're going that way." I glanced in the rear-view mirror and smiled at Carlito. "Ask him if he's hungry."

That question, when translated, got an enthusiastic nod. So Randy went to the kitchen to whip up a few more turkey sandwiches. Then he relinquished the couch to Carlito so he could take a nap, and rejoined me. "How are you doing?" he asked.

"Fine."

"Rattled?"

I laughed quietly. "I was, back there. You sure don't get that kind of excitement in Lawrenceburg, Indiana."

"Rick missed a good time, didn't he?"

My smile faded. "Yeah. Yeah, he did." I looked over at him. "I'm glad you here were with me. Thank you."

He shrugged. "Happy to be of service."

I was quiet for a few moments, thinking about how narrowly I'd avoided charring all five of those guys. It really *had* been a good thing that Randy was with me.

He got up and went to the pile of firearms I'd dumped behind my seat when I got in. "What are you doing?" I asked.

"Pulling the clips." He put the ammunition magazines in one pile and the guns in another. "We should store them in different places." He glanced at a snoozing Carlito as he spoke.

"You don't think he'd turn on us, do you?"

"Nope. But his brother's employer may decide he wants his guns back."

I felt a chill down my spine. "You think they'll follow us?" I checked the mirrors on either side of the RV. "Maybe we should turn everything over to the police and let them handle it."

"Bad idea," said Randy. "Mexican cops are notorious for being on the take. Let's wait 'til we get to Mexico City. Maybe Tim's girlfriend's family will know what to do with them."

I wasn't crazy about the idea, but I didn't have a better one.

Randy took over the driving around 10:00 p.m. I was nervous about stopping – I was still worried about the drug lord being on our tail – but my eyes were drooping shut every few minutes. The last thing I wanted was for us to get into a wreck in the dark.

The swap took about thirty seconds; I didn't even shut off the engine. Once out of the driver's seat, I sagged onto the dinette bench, nearly too tired to hoist myself up into bed.

My gaze fell on Carlito, who was still asleep with his back to me. I dragged myself upright again and went forward. "Hey, Randy?" I asked quietly.

"Yeah?"

"You know when I told the bad guys to leave Carlito alone, and my bird lit up?"

"Yeah?"

"He yelled something. A name, maybe. What was it?"

"Huitzilopochtli."

The name rang a bell from one of my college archaeology courses. "Refresh my memory. He is…?"

He glanced over his shoulder at me. "The Aztec sun god. He can take the form of an eagle."

"Ah. It was an honest mistake, then." I paused. "Is that why he thought I was a goddess?"

"No," Randy said, surprised. "It's because you barely touched his brother's buddy and nearly broke his arm."

I nodded. "That makes more sense. Thanks."

Randy glanced over his shoulder at me. "Get some sleep, Maggie."

"Good thinking. Goodnight." And I climbed up into bed without even changing into my pajamas.

Chapter 16

My sleep was deep and nearly dreamless. The one dream I had, I could have done without.

In it, I saw Rick standing before a turquoise-colored door. The door opened, revealing a woman with long, dark hair. She looked surprised, then delighted. Then she threw her arms around Rick's neck; his embrace was equally enthusiastic. Then she led him inside by the hand and closed the door behind them both.

I awoke with a lump in my throat and lay there for a moment, trying to forget what I'd seen. Gradually, I realized how bright it was around me. I pulled back the curtain on Rick's side of the bed and saw nothing but buildings and pavement, instead of the jagged mountains and scrubby plants I'd been used to seeing in the north.

I hadn't meant to sleep so long. I flipped over and scrambled down from the bunk. As I turned, I caught sight of Carlito at the dinette, frozen in place, with a spoonful of cereal halfway to his mouth. I smiled at him and gave him my best *buenos días*. I knew my accent was abysmal, but somehow he understood me.

"Buenos días, Doña Diosa," he replied with a grin.

There was that word again. I fled the two steps to the front of the RV. Leaning over the console, I asked Randy, "What time is it? Are we here?"

"Yeah," he said, bleary-eyed. "What's your son's address?"

"Why don't you pull over?" I said. "I can take it from here."

"Thank you," he said gratefully, and signaled to change lanes.

"How come you didn't wake me up?" I asked as we made the swap.

He mopped his face with one hand, then stretched. "You had a big day yesterday. I figured you needed the sleep."

"I appreciate that," I said, more tartly than I meant to. "But that's no reason to risk running us off the road."

"Well, it's too late now," he said. "I'm going to grab a bite with Carlito here, and then take a little nap."

"All right. But would you talk to him? He called me a goddess again a minute ago."

I glanced at him as I adjusted the rear-view mirror, and saw him smirking. "I heard."

I rolled my eyes. "Just talk to him."

Still grinning, he stepped toward the dinette.

Tim had an apartment in Coyoacán, not far from the University of Mexico's main campus. Thank goodness for cellular service and GPS apps – I would have been completely lost otherwise.

We parked the rig on the street in front of Tim's building, and the three of us – the old white woman, the Navajo man, and the Mexican youth – got out. I went first, and looked between the guys as they stepped out the door. It struck me that Randy could pass for Carlito's father in certain neighborhoods up north. Their skin tone and hair color were similar, although their faces were very different: Randy's was longer and leaner, while Carlito's nose and lips were broad.

I'd learned a few words of Spanish by now. So when Carlito pointed at the back of the RV and said, *"¡Mira!"* I knew I was supposed to look at something. The next word, however, I didn't know.

"What's he saying?" I said to Randy, who was already walking to where Carlito stood. He turned his head to look where the boy was pointing, and I saw his mouth drop open. I was already in motion by the time he beckoned to me.

"What'd he say?" I asked again. Then I looked, and took a breath.

"La telaraña," Randy said. "A spider's web."

A beautifully-wrought spider's web, in fact – stretching all across the back of the RV, from each corner of the bumper to the roof. "Was it there all night?" I asked, staring. "How did it stay intact?"

"Magic," Randy said.

"*Ella hace mágica*," Carlito said, nodding emphatically. "*Es diosa. Diosa de las arañas.*"

I had a pretty good idea of what he'd just said, even without asking Randy to translate. "I am not a goddess," I said, at my wit's end. "Please stop saying that!"

"Were you gonna come in, Mom?" asked Tim, coming down the walk toward us. "Or were you just gonna stand out here and stare at your RV all day?"

"Tim!" I hugged him hard, suddenly teary. I hadn't realized how tense I'd been for the past two days until I saw my son and realized we'd made it.

"How was the trip?" he asked, stepping back at last. "Any trouble? I see you picked up a buddy." He shook hands in turn with Randy and Carlito, and a conversation in Spanish ensued. I heard *mamá* a number of times, and *diosa* more than once.

"Would you please make him stop saying that?" I pleaded with Tim.

"Why?" Tim teased. "Aren't you flattered?"

"No," I said flatly.

Carlito broke in with an enthusiastic retelling of our adventure south of Torreón, including enough pantomime that I could follow him easily. As he spoke, Tim led us inside his apartment.

I could immediately see Ana's touch. The furnishings were spare, but the place was neat and clean. Among the decorations was a photo of the Virgin of Guadalupe in a tin frame. "Is Ana Catholic?" I asked my son.

"Nominally." He smiled slyly. "Her parents want us to get married in the church."

"Congratulations!" I beamed and hugged him again. "Where is she?"

"Gone to fetch her mother. She wants to meet you, too."

"Oh." I glanced down at the clothes I'd slept in, and put a hand to my bedhead hairdo. I had never even bothered to run a comb through my hair. "Maybe I'd better change first."

I had just enough time to pull myself together before Ana arrived, together with her mother and grandmother. Ana was adorable, with dark eyes, pale skin, and a cute figure. She spoke English, thank goodness. The guys had kept up their conversation in Spanish, and I had begun to feel lost.

Ana's mother was just as lovely, and very gracious. Her English was as bad as my Spanish, but we managed to exchange a few sentences.

Ana's grandmother, however, eyed me with suspicion. While Ana encouraged her to come and meet me, the old woman muttered the word *bruja*. Ana reared back in alarm, and exchanged a look of panic with her mother.

"What does that mean?" I asked Randy, who had caught the exchange.

He lowered his voice. "She thinks you're a witch."

"That's just great," I said. "Between Carlito and Ana's granny, I've got both good and evil covered."

When I said the boy's name, Ana's mother perked up. She stared at him for a moment. "Carlito?" she said. "Carlito Martinez?"

The boy had been deep in conversation with Tim, but turned at the sound of his name. He spied Ana's mother and cried, "*¡Tía Alicia!*" The next thing I knew, both mother and grandmother were embracing and kissing him.

I leaned toward Randy. "What are the odds that our Carlito would be related to Ana?"

"Pretty low," he said. "Must be magic."

It turned out that one of Ana's many siblings, Guillermo, was an officer in the Mexican army. When he came for dinner at Ana's parents' house that night, he was very interested indeed to hear Carlito's story, and he vowed to speak to those higher up his chain of command to see whether the boy's older brother couldn't be rescued, too. "Since El Chapo was arrested two years ago, all the minor drug lords in northern Mexico have been jockeying to be number one," Tim told us. "It's been a no-man's land up there. That's why I was so hesitant when you wanted to drive down here – I knew something might go wrong."

"Something did go wrong," I said. "I should have listened to you – and to Rick."

"But Mom, don't you see? This was a stroke of luck. Guillermo thinks the military will be able to exploit Carlito's inside knowledge of this particular operation and put a criminal behind bars. You did a good thing by driving down and rescuing him."

"I'm glad you think so," I said.

Tim regarded me with compassion. "Have you heard from him?"

I knew who he meant. "No." I sucked in a breath. "And I don't expect to. Not until I'm back in the States, if then."

Ana called Tim's name, and he smiled and waved to her. "You'll have to tell me later what happened," he said, getting up.

"Sure," I said with a weak smile, even though I had no idea what to tell him. I hardly knew what had happened myself. And the dream vision I'd had of Rick in another woman's arms haunted me.

That wasn't the only thing haunting me.

Carlito's aunt and uncle took him home with them after dinner. Ana went with them. Tim didn't have a guest room – the only available extra sleeping space was the living room sofa – so he gallantly gave up his and Ana's room so I could have my own space. Randy was happy to keep bunking in the RV, and was also happy to have a full-size bathroom with a shower, instead of the tiny quarters inside the rig.

It seemed no sooner than I had said good night to my son and laid my head upon the pillow, I was hijacked by a vision.

It started the same as the last few I'd had: spidery petroglyphs had wrapped me in silken bonds and were dragging me through the streets. I recognized the iconic classroom building of the University of Mexico as we hurtled along. Above us, a bird flew silently on outspread wings. A

Thunderbird? No, I could feel my bird quiescent against my chest. An eagle, then. No – an owl. I saw her face clearly as she turned to look at me.

Our journey seemed to take forever, but at last we arrived at an archaeological site: a wide avenue flanked by pyramids and the bases of former structures. Before me was a small pyramid, cut away to reveal a temple underneath, with what might have been a reflecting pool before it. Farther along to my left was a huge pyramid, easily seven hundred feet across at the base, the sides ringed with terraces at uneven intervals. Most of the surviving structures, I noticed, were built in a similar terraced style. And at the end of the road was another large pyramid, shorter than the biggest but nearly as broad at the base, with a wide staircase leading to a platform at the top. Its overall shape mimicked the mountain behind it.

This shorter pyramid – or rather, the plaza in front of it – was our destination. As the spiders continued to pull me along, the owl I'd seen earlier landed in the middle of the plaza and changed into a woman before my eyes. She retained her owl-like eyes, but her face was yellow, and she wore massive headgear that looked for all the world as if a tree were growing out of the middle of it. The spiders let go of me and swarmed over her as if she were their mother.

"At last," she said, her voice booming in my head. She spoke neither English nor Spanish, but I understood every word she said. "Come closer, Nokomtha."

The webbing had dissolved when the spiders deserted me, I guessed. I walked forward unencumbered.

"Hmm," she said. "Yes, I see why Kokumthena chose you. But you have one lesson yet to learn." And she raised her hands, allowing water to pour from her sleeves.

I watched, fascinated, as the water level in the plaza rose. I should have been frightened, but something told me I was in no danger of drowning. The water was not the thing I should fear here.

No, that would be the snakes that slithered from her sleeves into the water. Many, many snakes. Snakes that grew rapidly in size, until they were as big around as a dolphin and many times larger. Feathered ruffs encircled their necks. They surrounded me, bumping up against me as they glided past.

I stood transfixed by fear. They reminded me far too much of the Underwater Panther.

The goddess – for I was sure she had to be one – laughed at my reaction, but her laughter was kind. "Do not be afraid, Nokomtha! These feathered serpents are our friends. See how they accompany the life-giving water that sustains us and allows our plants to grow." And without leaving the spot where I stood, I became aware that I was seeing the scene from far above. This ancient site was near several watercourses, and someone had built canals from them to irrigate nearby fields.

"But water can be dangerous, too," I said.

"Yes, it can. Like all elements, it can help and harm, cleanse and inundate. Create and destroy." The water level in the plaza began to rise; it was soon above my waist and still rising. I tried to flee, but my feet seemed anchored to the pavement. "Make it stop!" I screeched. "I'll drown!"

"You will be cleansed," she said reassuringly. "You will be remade."

In a panic, I tried desperately to swim away. But it was no use – I was stuck, and the water kept rising. I held my breath as it rose above the level of my mouth, then my nose, then the crown of my head – but at last I could hold it no longer. I sent a mental goodbye to my children and to Rick, released my spent air, and gulped the water down.

The feathered serpents sluiced through every part of me – my heart and lungs, my bowels, my extremities – until they filled each crack and crevice. Then the water they arrived in drained away through every orifice and pore. With it went all the pain I'd endured over the past few months: the grief from losing my mother, the anger at Sandy, the despair over what Gene had done to my children and me, and the betrayal at Rick's abrupt departure. I understood now that it had all been necessary. All of it. It had created the crucible in which I had been tempered. As fire had burned away the worst of my external hurts, now water washed away the internal debris.

But the water serpents stayed behind. They were part of me now, melded into my every cell. Or more accurately, they had always been part of me – as natural and as needful as skin and bone and blood. It was as I had always feared: the Water Serpent, the Destroyer, was as much a part of me as the Creator. And it was okay. I was okay. This was the way it was supposed to be.

The plaza was bone-dry. I stood upon the dirt and filled my lungs with air. "Thank you," I said to the goddess who still stood before me.

She laughed. "Do not think we are done. I have granted you a boon, Nokomtha. I have finished the work Kokumthena began in you. Now you must grant a boon to us in return."

I straightened. "Name it."

She smiled, revealing curved teeth that resembled a spider's mouthparts. "She *has* chosen well," she said. Then she sobered. "A long time ago – centuries, by human reckoning – a great harm was done to the people known as the Shawnee."

"The American government removed them from their ancestral lands and sent them west," I said. "Most tribes in America suffered the same fate."

"The great harm I speak of happened long before," she said. "The people who became known as the Shawnee lived here in Mexico first."

"Oh?" This was news to me.

"For thousands of years, they made their home near Lake Chapala, west of this place. But the Nahua peoples moved down from their homeland in the north, which they called Aztlán, and were determined to conquer as much land as they could."

"Aztlán?" I said. "I thought that was the mythical homeland of the Aztecs."

"The Aztecs were a Nahua tribe," she said. "And they conquered other tribes by slavery and slaughter. The Shawnee refused to bend the knee to the Nahua. They endured, but eventually they could endure no more. They escaped by crossing Mexico to the Yucatán peninsula and traveling from there to their new home. Half the tribe went by land around the Gulf of Mexico, and the other half crossed the gulf by boat."

"When was this?"

"Around three thousand years ago."

I did the math. "They must have stopped at Cahokia," I said. "Or some of them did." I remembered, then, the sense of familiar fear I'd felt outside of Monks Mound. "Did the Nahua follow them?"

"They were not following the Shawnee, but a Nahua tribe did attempt to take over Cahokia in its final days."

I felt again that old fear and animosity, and shuddered. Then I said, "What would you have me do?"

"This rift between the Nahua and the Shawnee has never been healed. Kokumthena and I would see our peoples united. This you must do for us."

"I will," I said. "But how?"

"It will require blood," she intoned.

I stepped back. "Sacrifice?" I said. "Oh, no. We're modern people. We don't do blood sacrifices any more."

"Blood must be spilled," she said. "Blood must be joined for the rift to mend." She turned and pointed at the pyramid behind her. "There. As in days of old."

I shook my head in horror. "I can't do that."

"You must!" she shouted. Thunder reverberated, and the spiders chittered around me...

I woke up with my heart pounding, and fumbled around on Tim's bedside table until I found the switch for his reading light. I turned it on. It didn't help.

Who was this spirit? And did she actually expect me to kill...?

My gaze fell on a photo Tim had framed and placed next to his bed. It was a selfie of him and Ana, wearing dazzling smiles. Behind them loomed the pyramid I'd just seen in my dream.

I turned off the light and lay back down, even though I knew I wouldn't sleep any more that night.

I felt clearer than I had before my psychic near-drowning, but I began to wish the goddess hadn't bothered to grant me her boon. Again, I wished I'd listened to Rick and flown to Mexico City – or never come here at all.

But if I hadn't come, I wouldn't have met Ana or her family. And if we hadn't driven down, Carlito would still be a prisoner of the drug lord, and his brother would have no hope of rescue. I was glad to have had a hand in all of that. But would the price be too high for me to pay?

Did she really expect me to kill…?

Granny-as-Kokumthena had told me, when all this began, that once all six doors had closed against me, *then, and only then, will the right door open. When that occurs, you must walk through, and quickly, for it will not stay open long.*

Was this the open door? This healing of an ancient wound between two Indian tribes? How could that possibly lead me to the rest of my life?

I lay there until the sky began to lighten. Then I picked up the photo frame and went out into the living room.

Tim was already up and getting ready to go for a run. "Good morning," he said as he tied his shoes. "Feel free to make yourself some coffee."

I sat down next to him on the couch and showed him the photo. "Where was this taken?"

"Isn't it a great photo?" he said. "That's at Teotihuacán. I told you we went there, remember? It was just before I flew up to Maryland to stay with Nana."

"I remember. What's the name of the thing behind you?"

"That's the Pyramid of the Moon," he said. "The people who built it used to make blood sacrifices on those stairs."

I shivered. "Go for your run," I said. "And when you get back, you need to tell me everything you remember about what you and Ana experienced at Teotihuacán."

Chapter 17

Two days later, Tim, Ana, Randy, and I were on our way to Teotihuacán. Ana's grandmother – the woman who'd called me a witch when we first arrived – insisted on coming with us. Ana called her Abuelita, which I learned meant "little grandmother"; Tim called her Doña Meztli, so that's what I called her, too.

Ana picked up Tim, Randy, and me not long after sunrise. Traffic in Mexico City is as bad as in any other big city, and Ana wanted to get a jump on it. As we piled into the back seat of her car, I was surprised to see Carlito sitting between Ana and her grandmother. He grinned and waved at me.

Ana said, "When he heard you were coming, Doña Brandt, he insisted on coming, too."

I reached forward and patted him on the shoulder. "I'm glad he's here," I said, although I wasn't sure if that was true. I'd figured on just Tim, Ana, and me, with Randy as witness to what I had to do. It was going to be hard enough to accomplish in a public place – spectators would make us even more of, well, a spectacle.

The drive took a couple of hours, which gave Tim and Ana plenty of time to explain again – in English and Spanish – what they'd experienced on their first visit to Teotihuacán. They had climbed the Pyramid of the Sun first, and then the Pyramid of the Moon. Tim had described the sensation he felt at the top of the Pyramid of the Sun as a loosening of something inside him. Ana, he'd said, had felt the same sensation. And he said whatever had been loosened had been undergone a realignment as they climbed the Pyramid of the Moon.

"At first I thought it was just about us," Tim said, reaching forward to touch Ana's shoulder. She smiled and put her hand over his for a moment. "But then you told me about your experience in the Great Circle, Mom. And I began to think the two experiences were related."

"You could be right," I said, and explained what the goddess had told me in my early morning vision.

I hadn't gotten far into the telling when Carlito, to whom Ana was giving a play-by-play, got very excited. He had an extended conversation with Tim, Ana, and Doña Meztli that I couldn't understand – although I caught the word *bruja* a couple of times, and *diosa* several more.

"What are you saying?" I said at last, a touch irritably.

"Sorry," Tim said. "Carlito believes you were visited by the Great Goddess."

"La Gran Diosa de Teotihuacán," Carlito said, nodding. "La Gran Diosa de Arañas."

"Spider Woman," said Randy in dawning comprehension.

"Okay, somebody clue me in," I said sharply.

Randy said, "Remember when I told you about Spider Rock?"

"The spire at Canyon de Chelly? Sure. Oh." Now I made the connection. "So this Great Goddess, whoever she is, is the same as your Spider Woman. Or similar, anyway."

"I don't think they're exactly the same deity," said Tim, "but they have a lot of similarities. Spider Woman is a creator figure. The Great Goddess of Teotihuacán is more along the lines of Kali."

"Creator and destroyer, right?" I said, brushing off the dust on my scanty knowledge of Hindu deities. "That does tally with what the Great Goddess told me in my vision. Who is she, anyway?"

"One of the major deities worshipped by the Teotihuacanos," Tim said. "There's an amazing mural of her at Tetitla. We'll stop there on our way to the pyramids."

"For a long time," Ana said, "archaeologists believed Tlaloc, the god of rain, was the most important deity in the Teotihuacano pantheon. The murals and statues of the Great Goddess were all assumed to be statues of Tlaloc until someone noticed they were wearing a dress." She smirked.

"Sounds like a bunch of guys to me," I said.

She grinned at me in the rear-view mirror. "Even now, it is hard for some of them to believe that the Teotihuacanos' most important deity could be female. Many believe the Great Goddess and Tlaloc were worshipped together as a couple, even though many more depictions of the Great Goddess have been found."

We arrived at Teotihuacán so early that we nearly had the place to ourselves. And Tim was right: the mural of the Great Goddess at Tetitla was amazing. "That's her, all right," I said, noting the serpent and wave patterns on her sleeves, the tree in her headdress, and the spider-like teeth. "Is she associated with owls, too?"

"Yep," Tim said. "See the goggles she's wearing? And she's also associated with jaguars."

I was grateful I hadn't met up with any jaguars in my vision.

As we made our way toward the Avenue of the Dead – the ancient main street that connects all of the ceremonial sites in Teotihuacán – I began to feel that old, familiar pull. "This way," I said, turning left.

"Don't you want to see the whole avenue?" Tim asked. " I thought we'd start with the Palace of Quetzalcoatl, since it's right here, and work our way north."

"Maybe later," I said. "Come on." I headed up the avenue for a few hundred feet, and then realized no one was with me. I turned to see them all standing in a gaggle, staring at me. "Come on!" I urged, and strode off again.

"There's no arguing with her when she gets like this," I heard Randy say.

"Yeah, I know," said Tim.

I glanced over my shoulder and saw them hurrying after me. Satisfied, I turned back and let my intuition guide me – straight ahead, toward the Pyramid of the Moon.

Someone slid a hand into mine. I looked over, then down. It was Carlito, keeping pace with me. I smiled and squeezed his hand, and together we forged ahead.

I hope you don't think I knew what I was doing. I'd thought long and hard about what the goddess wanted me to accomplish, and frankly I had no idea how I was going to accomplish it. I was pretty sure Tim and Ana were necessary, but I couldn't see how they would fit. I was supposed to heal a rift between two Indian tribes by spilling somebody's blood. You'd think it would be necessary to have someone from each of those tribes present.

I looked at Carlito. "Are...*tú*..." I pointed at him. "Aztec?" He gave me a blank look. I tried again. "Nahua? *Méxica?*"

He gave me a surprised grin and jammed the thumb of his free hand at his heart. "*¡Sí! ¡Soy Méxica!*"

"And Ana?"

"*Claro. Ana es Méxica también,*" he replied.

I got what I needed out of that. Ana could stand in for the Nahua. Or Carlito could. Or Doña Meztli, I supposed. But I was still short a Shawnee.

And then I remembered Randy's suggestion that maybe I had more Indian in me than I thought. Not just a soul tie to a Hopewell shaman, but actual Native American blood in my family tree.

I supposed it could be possible. My parents both said their families had always lived in Indiana, ever since its frontier days. It wasn't outside the realm of possibility that some ancestor had married a Shawnee, way back when.

Under my shirt, my turtle began dancing.

Carlito's eyes bugged out at the party going on in there, so I pulled out the necklace and let it hang free. I hadn't been paying much attention to my effigies since we'd picked him up; they'd been quiet, and I'd had a lot of other things on my mind. But now I noticed the turtle had been cleaning herself up when I wasn't looking. The stubborn green-and-black tarnish was nearly all gone; the original copper surface shone. And she was still twitching on her chain, clinking against my bird, which was beginning to grow warm.

I hoped the bird wouldn't put on a show. A fire was the last thing we needed right now.

But what had set the turtle off? I'd been thinking about whether I had any Shawnee blood...

The turtle rattled again in confirmation.

Well, okay. If I were Shawnee, then Tim was, too. And Ana was Nahua. So I had my sacrificial victims. Now I just had to figure out how to get a sufficient amount of blood out of them without killing them.

The Teotihuacanos didn't have any qualms about the killing part. Another mural at Tetitla showed how it had been done: priests led a line of victims to the Pyramid of the Moon, then cut them up. Their blood ran down the steps in a torrent that drained into a stream or canal, where it turned into life-giving water for plants. Some people died so that the rest could go on living.

Which worked splendidly until the land fell into drought, as sometimes happens. It had at Cahokia, and Tim had mentioned that it had here, too. Both civilizations had ended in upheaval – looting and fire. There was speculation that the common folks, starving and disillusioned, had overthrown the elite themselves.

The rest of the gang had long since caught up with Carlito and me. I glanced toward the west, where clouds were massing. "Is it supposed to rain today?" I asked Tim.

"Maybe," he said, looking west. "I don't think so, though."

"We'd better get this over with before we get drenched," I muttered, and picked up my pace. I'd had enough of drowning on the Great Goddess's orders.

Up the stairs we climbed. There weren't a lot of them, as these things go, but Mexico City is more than seven thousand feet high to start with, and the steps at the Pyramid of the Moon are steep. I would have had to crawl up the last several steps if Carlito hadn't been there to help me.

Doña Meztli, I noticed, didn't have any trouble with the climb. I put it down to acclimation to the altitude.

At the top, I looked around while I concentrated on catching my breath. The view itself is breathtaking, down the full length of the Avenue of the Dead.

Ana looked at me and smiled. Then she glanced down at my necklace, which I'd forgotten to tuck back inside my shirt. "Oh," she said faintly, and reached for it.

The bird flew up of its own accord and sliced open the palm of her hand.

At her gasp of shock, Tim came to her side. "What happened?" he asked, cradling her injured hand in one of his. And the bird struck again, cutting into his thumb.

"Ow!" he said. "Mom!" And he made to put his thumb in his mouth.

"No! Turn it over!" I said.

Tim looked at me crossly. "What?"

I grabbed both of their hands and dragged them to the steps. "Mix your blood together," I said, pressing his thumb into her palm. "There. Now." I turned their injured hands over and waited until several drops of blood made a small puddle on the top stair.

Thunder rumbled.

I looked up. The clouds had moved in, almost too fast to be natural. Lightning lanced the sky, and thunder boomed a few moments later.

"Welcome, Thunderbird," I said, a tad ironically. "Thanks for the help."

"Come on," Randy said, one hand on my elbow. "We're targets for that lightning up here."

"Good point," I said, handing Tim and Ana each a tissue for their cuts. Then I tucked my necklace back inside my shirt, where my effigies couldn't hurt anyone but me, and we hurtled down the steps.

We didn't make it. The storm was too close. Before we'd covered half the distance to the Pyramid of the Sun, the skies opened. We were soaked well before we got back to the visitors center.

"Well, it worked," I said as we stood inside the doors and dripped all over their flooring. "We made the sacrifice and the rains came."

Randy paused in the act of wringing out a corner of his t-shirt to grin at me. "Magic," he said.

"¡*Mira!*" said Carlito, pointing at my shoulder. I glanced over and saw a spider – not a petroglyph, a real one – dropping from above on a line of silk. It hovered for a moment, then dropped to the floor.

"You're welcome," I said as it skittered out of sight.

"Maggie May?"

I wheeled around, and there by the door stood Rick. Wordlessly, I threw myself into his arms.

Of all the miracles I'd seen that day, that one was the best.

Chapter 18

The thunderstorm moved out as rapidly as it had moved in, leaving Teotihuacán freshly-washed but muddy. Tim proposed that we see the rest of the complex anyway, as long as we were here. Our whole group left the visitor center together, but the others soon outpaced Rick and me.

We walked hand-in-hand, caring less about the archaeological wonders around us than we did about the physical contact. And the catching up.

I brought him up to speed pretty quickly: our rescue of Carlito, my dream visit with the Great Goddess, and the blood sacrifice on the steps of the Pyramid of the Moon just a few minutes before.

"Missed it by that much," he said, doing a fair imitation of Don Adams' character in the old *Get Smart* TV show. That got a laugh out of me. Then he sighed dramatically. "Story of my life."

"True enough," I said, teasing.

"So you're part Shawnee?"

I shrugged. "We must be. Otherwise the blood bond wouldn't have worked the way it did."

He glanced up at the Pyramid of the Moon. "I suppose it's no use going to find the evidence. The rain would have washed it all away."

"Yup. It worked exactly the way it was supposed to. But it explains why I had that visceral reaction at Cahokia. Some of the Shawnee must have made a stop there on their way to Ohio. They would have known exactly what was coming when the Nahua showed up."

"Seems plausible."

I swung his hand back and forth a couple of times. "So…"

"My turn?"

I nodded. I couldn't bring myself to ask about the woman I'd seen him with.

He cleared his throat. "Well. I didn't go back home."

"Oh?"

"No." He gave me a quick, nervous glance. "I went to see Belinda."

I kept my voice level and willed my hand not to tighten around his. "Oh? Why?"

"Well, since I was in the neighborhood," he said with a weak chuckle. When I didn't reply, he said, "I felt like I needed to get some things straight with her."

The silence that followed was maddening. "Am I going to have to pry this out of you, word by word?" I asked, exasperated. "Just spit it out already."

He stopped in surprise. "You think I...? Oh, no, Maggie May. I'm not interested in getting back together with her. That horse has left the barn." He resumed walking. "If anything, seeing her again made me more certain of that than ever. But we'd parted badly."

"Divorce does that," I said.

"It does. But time has a way of mellowing those emotions, if you let it." He chuckled. "She even hugged me. I didn't think she'd ever do that again."

Yes, I saw it. But I kept that to myself. "So was your conversation productive, then?"

He nodded. "Uh-huh. We've both moved on. Found others we care about." He glanced at me warily. "We talked about you."

My gut clenched. "About me?" I managed.

"Well, you were on my mind for some reason." His mouth quirked up at the corners. "And she said a very wise thing. She said, 'Rick, don't be a moron. You've loved this woman forever. Go back to her and work it out.' So I changed my ticket and came here."

I pulled him to a stop. "Wait. How long is forever?"

"Since high school," he admitted. "At least."

"Why didn't you ever *tell* me?"

"It was dumb," he said. "*I* was dumb. And young. I guess I was waiting for a signal from you."

"I wasn't just dumb. I was oblivious." I thought back over the years of our friendship. "My God, Rick. No wonder you hated Gene."

"Well, now," he said, wagging a finger at me, "I was right about that."

I laughed. "You were. Still. My life would have been so different if I'd married you instead of him."

He nodded toward Tim and Ana, who had separated from the rest of the group, too. "You wouldn't have your kids."

"I'd have different kids," I said.

His mouth worked for a moment. "I wanted kids," he said at last.

I slid my arms around his waist. "You can share mine."

After we got back to Tim's, we reclaimed the RV from Randy. "If it's rockin', I won't come knockin'," he said, handing over the keys.

"Ha ha," I said.

"This is better all the way around," he said. "I don't mind sleeping on the couch, so Tim gets his room back. And you'll quit moping."

"Moping!" I said in mock outrage.

"I'm really glad you're back," Randy said to Rick, who was appreciating this conversation a little too much. "I couldn't take much more of it. She's been horrible to be around. Always staring off into space and letting out these big sighs." He nudged Rick with an elbow. "You know how women are."

"I don't think I'd push her if I were you," Rick said. "She's got some pretty hefty firepower under her shirt there."

Randy's eyes danced. "You're the one who'd know."

Later that night – after the RV had quit rockin' – I gazed at the effigies in the dim light and wondered what state my turtle would have been in if I had never moved to Maryland. What if Rick and I had gotten together sooner? Would I have earned that degree in archaeology? Maybe gone on to grad school? I might have worked on a dig at the Newark Earthworks, or at Serpent Mound. I still would have been knocked off my true path –

Mom and Sandy had seen to that – but I might have found my way back sooner with Rick in my corner.

There was no use wondering about what could have been. All I could do now was to stay on the path, now that I'd found it again.

My turtle rattled softly in agreement.

I dreamed I was in a store full of music boxes. I opened box after box, looking for the tune that was mine, but they all played the same one.

Ruth stood at my side, looking as she had when my kids were small. "Take this one," she said.

I looked at it and shook my head. It was shaped exactly like her house. "I told you before, I don't want it," I said.

"But listen," she said. "It's playing your song." She pulled up the roof on one side, and the most beautiful melody came out. "Now take it! I have to go!" And she shoved the box into my hand.

The roof fell back into place, but the music kept playing. Over and over.

I raised my head from the pillow and realized I'd incorporated the ringing of my cell phone into the dream. I fumbled for the phone on the shelf above my head. "Hello?"

"Maggie!" Riley said, relief flooding her voice. "Thank God. I've been calling and calling you!"

I slid out from under Rick's arm across my waist and tried to climb out of the bunk while holding the phone. No good. "Hang on," I said, and put down the phone so I could get down without falling on my butt. Then I picked up the phone. "Okay. Sorry. What's going on?"

"Ruth had a heart attack," she said.

I sank down on a dinette bench. *I have to go.* "Oh, no," I said. "When was this?"

"A few hours ago," she said. "I think. I'd set her alarm because she had an appointment with John today. I kept hearing the alarm buzzing, and finally I went in to check on her, and she wouldn't wake up."

"My God," I said. "I'm so sorry, Riley."

"Thanks," she said automatically. "Anyway, I'm at the hospital now."

"Have you talked with John?" I asked.

"Oh!" she said. "I need to cancel her appointment, don't I?"

I realized she was as much in shock as Ruth was. "Is John with her right now?"

"Yeah, I called him at home. They're gonna charge her for the appointment, aren't they?"

"Riley," I said. "I want you to sit down and take three breaths. Deep and slow. Just breathe. Okay?"

"Okay." I heard her gasp.

"Slower," I said, and counted for her – in for five beats, out for ten. The last thing she needed was to hyperventilate and pass out. On the other hand, I reflected, she was in the perfect place to recover if she did.

"Okay," she said. "Thanks, Maggie. That helps."

"Good. Do you want me to come out to help?"

"Maybe. I… Oh, wait. Here comes John. I'll call you back." And the line went dead.

"It's Ruth," said Rick from the bed.

I nodded. "Heart attack. I need to tell Tim."

As I reached for the doorknob, he laughed. "Not like that, you're not."

I looked down and realized I'd shed my pajama pants at some point in the night. I looked at him, side-eyed. "I should probably get dressed first, huh?"

He slid out of bed himself, took two steps, and wrapped his arms around me. "Maybe not," he said, and kissed me.

Things hadn't gotten very far along when my phone rang again. I gave him a lingering kiss and said, "Don't lose my place." Then I answered the phone.

"She's gone," Riley said tonelessly. "What do I do now?"

Rick, Tim, and I flew from Mexico City to BWI the next day. Ana couldn't come, as she had yet to get a visa to enter the United States. "We were waiting 'til after we got married," Tim said, "so she'd have a better chance of getting one without a hassle."

The big question was what to do with the RV. Initially, Rick offered to drive it back to Indiana – but then Randy stepped up. "I don't have any other way to get home," he said. "I'll drive it."

"I'll talk to Guillermo," Tim said. "I bet his guys will give you an escort to the border."

"That would be great. I could use their help with the *federales*, since it's not my vehicle."

"This is very kind of you," I said. "We can come to New Mexico and pick it up after the funeral."

"Oh, no," Randy said. "I'd rather deliver it to you, wherever you are. I've got the travel bug now. I want to see Cahokia and the Great Circle. And I want to stand in Kokumthena's forest."

"Sounds like a win-win," Rick said as I handed over the keys.

The flight to BWI was a lot shorter than our drive had been – and much, much shorter than the Shawnees' journey to Ohio. I stared out over the Gulf of Mexico and thought about what it must have been like to shove off from the Yucatan in primitive boats, not knowing where they'd end up. It had taken them years to find where they belonged.

I turned to look at Rick beside me. He was snoring softly, his mouth slightly open. It was a horribly undignified pose for a guy who'd once made his living as a criminal defense lawyer. I could not have loved him more.

John picked us up at the airport. "We could have grabbed an Uber," Tim said as we got in the car.

"You're welcome," John said, slapping him on the knee. "Where are you guys staying?"

"Drop us at Ruth's," I said. "I want to see how Riley is doing."

Riley was not doing well at all. I still had a key to Ruth's place, so I let us in without knocking. We found Riley sitting cross-legged on the floor of Debbie's old room with packing crates around her.

"What are you doing?" I said.

"Maggie!" She jumped to her feet and hugged me. "I'm so glad you're here. Hi, Tim." She moved on to give my son – her stepson – a hug, and gave Rick one for good measure. Then she stepped back. "I just don't know where to start."

"Start at the beginning," I said.

"No, with the house," she said. "We're going to have to get rid of all this stuff. But first I need to find another place to live." She flipped her long, dark hair back over one shoulder. I would not have thought it possible for Riley to get any thinner than she had been, but she looked like a waif, hollow-eyed, the bones at her neckline standing out in stark relief.

"Maybe," I said. "But we don't have to do any of that right now. Let's get past the funeral. Then we can figure the rest of this out." I hooked my thumb at the stairs. "Come on down and let's all have coffee or something. When did you eat last?"

"I dunno," she said, casting a glance toward the boxes.

"Let's get some food into you, too." I caught Tim's eye.

"Good idea," he said instantly. "I'm starving. I'll call Ledo's and order pizza." And he disappeared down the stairs.

Over square slices topped with pepperoni and mushroom, I got the whole story out of her. Ruth hadn't felt well the night before and had gone up to bed early. Riley had checked on her around midnight, realized she hadn't turned on her alarm, and took care of that. "I didn't check to see whether she was breathing," she said. "She might have been dead by then."

"But you told me she'd hit the snooze button at least once."

"Oh. Right. But she might have been in distress. I should have checked on her again." Riley stopped picking at her pizza and sat back, her hands twisting around each other.

"You need to stop looking for trouble," said Tim. "Did John say it was your fault?"

"No," she said, slumping. "He said it was a massive attack and there was nothing I could have done to save her. But he might have just *said* that."

"I'll ask him," I said. "Will that make you feel better?"

"Maybe."

"Riley," Rick said, "have you contacted Ruth's lawyer?"

"Bea's doing all that. I gave her all of the paperwork and stuff. She's making all the funeral arrangements, too." She wrung her hands again. "I told her I'd take care of packing up the house."

"Why are you in such a hurry?" I said. "I mean, we don't even know what the will says yet."

"I do," Riley said, looking at me. "I witnessed it. The lawyer said it was okay for me to sign it since I wasn't getting anything. Debbie and Abby get to pick whatever they want from the household stuff. She wrote Gene out of it after he screwed up at the rehab facility." She took obvious pleasure in saying that. "All the cash gets split among trusts for the grandkids."

"Bernice, too?" I asked.

"Yeah. And there's some set aside for Lenny, and for Tim's kids. If you ever have any," she said to him. "And there's a bequest to the synagogue, too." She resumed peeling pepperoni off her slice of pizza.

"Who gets the house?" I asked, even though I already knew.

Riley chewed the pepperoni and swallowed. "You do," she said, and blotted her lips with a napkin. "That's why I need to pack. I figured you'd sell it right away. I knew you didn't want it."

"Well, I've changed my mind," I said. "I'm not going back to Indiana and I need a home base. It might as well be here."

Riley's eyes grew wide. "Really?"

"Really. And I wouldn't kick you out, ever."

She burst out of her chair and threw her arms around my neck. "Thank you! Oh, God, I've been so *worried*. I don't have *anyplace* else to go."

I patted her on the back. "I know. Everything's going to be fine."

Riley hugged me again and resumed her seat, crossing her legs twice, knee and ankle. As she picked up her slice of pizza and took an enormous bite, I distinctly heard a door open. "Did someone come in just now?" I asked.

Tim got up and went to the foyer. "There's nobody there, Mom," he called on his way back to the kitchen. "You must be hearing things."

"Maybe it was Ruth's ghost," Riley said.

"I doubt it. She's long gone." I smiled, mostly to myself. "It must have been all in my head."

Chapter 19

Dusk was falling as I navigated the RV into a pull-through spot in the Newark Earthworks parking lot – the small one just off State Road 79, closest to the Great Circle. Then I turned the driver's seat around and groaned as I creaked upright. "It's rough, getting old," I told Rick as he sat at the dinette, working on his laptop.

"It ain't for sissies," he said, rising to meet me. "I guess Granny's not here yet."

"The van's not here, anyway," I said. "I'm not sure she needs it at this point."

"Zed can't travel at the speed of light, can he?" He put an arm around my shoulder and kissed me.

"I wouldn't put it past him," I said. "How's the will coming?"

He drew in a breath. "It's a little complicated, but not terribly so. I should have it ready by the time we get home."

I closed my eyes and smiled. Even nine years after Rick had sold his parents' old house in Lawrenceburg to move in with me in Rockville, I still savored the sound of *we* and *home* in the same sentence.

"You know what you have to do in there?" he asked.

"Nope. But winging it has gotten me this far. I'm not about to quit now."

Someone rapped on the door. "Maybe that's Granny," I said. Then I called out, "Come on in."

"The RV's not rockin' so I guess it's safe," said Randy as he entered, a gust of chilly air following him.

"Hey, there!" said Rick, shaking hands. "Good to see you. We wondered if you'd be here."

"Oh, I wouldn't miss this for the world," Randy said. "Do you know who else is coming?"

I slapped my forehead in mock consternation. "I knew I should have sent out RSVP cards."

"We'll just have to see who shows up," Rick said.

"As long as Granny's here," I said, "that's really all that matters. Come on, you guys." I shrugged on my coat and led the way.

Rick pulled up the collar of his jacket. "Why can't we move this major lunar standstill to a warmer time of year?" he asked. "I thought it lasted 'til May or something."

"Actually, it's visible for a couple of years, either side," Randy said. "I'm with him."

I rolled my eyes at them. "I'm just glad the skies are clear. We'll have a perfect view of the moon as it rises."

We entered the Great Circle through the gap in the earthen walls. As always, I marveled at the way the Hopewell had been able to build such a monument with nothing but bone tools and baskets to carry dirt.

A small group of people were already gathered near Eagle Mound near the center of the circle. "Oh, hey, it's Janie McClatchey!" Randy said. He walked ahead of Rick and me to shake hands with her. "Good to see you!"

I remembered her from Cahokia. "Hi," I said, and gave her a hug. "Thanks for coming."

"Wouldn't miss it," she said with a smile. "Is Granny here yet?"

"Not so far," I said.

"Hello, Maggie," a tall fellow said as he approached us.

"Dirk Benson," I said, and shook his hand. "Long time no see."

"Sorry. I've been absorbed in my work for the past several years." He puffed himself up a little. "I'm looking into the shaman's role in these types of phenomena. I'm thinking of publishing a paper on them."

"Uh-huh," said Randy, casting a significant look at me.

Needless to say, Dirk missed it. "I hope you'll be willing to share your insights with me after all this is over, Maggie."

"Of course." I smiled at him, and glanced at my phone for the time. "Now if you all will excuse me, I need to get ready. The ceremony starts when the moon rises over the hills over there." I pointed to the east, where a faint silver glow was visible on the horizon.

"We can't start without the guest of honor," Dirk said.

"She'll be here," I said. "I'm confident of that." I waved and walked up the slight rise to the top of Eagle Mound.

I hadn't been completely truthful with Rick – I did have some idea what was coming, thanks to a chat I'd had with Zed a few months before. It had been one of those January days in the mid-Atlantic when the weather gods suddenly decide to give us a taste of spring. I'd taken the opportunity to open all the windows in order to air out the house, and then went for a walk in Rock Creek Park.

I had gotten into the habit of walking there pretty often, and every time I passed the spot when, years ago, I'd thought I'd seen a Water Panther reach up and snatch a turtle off the bank, I smiled. The water serpents that were part of me would wiggle a little. I translated that as laughter. All those months I feared the Water Panther and thought it was evil, and it turned out it was just doing what it was meant to do.

We all have our roles to play.

On that January day, as I came out of the park, I saw Zed's ancient VW bus at the curb. I knocked and opened the sliding door on the side without prompting.

"Hey, Maggie," Zed said from his usual chair. He was dressed in his usual refugee-from-the-'60s attire: faded jeans, tie-dyed shirt, and a bandanna tied around his head. The couch where Granny usually sat was empty.

"Hey, Zed," I said, climbing in. "Where is she?"

"That's what I've come to talk to you about. Have a seat."

I eased myself into the other chair. "I know it's almost time for Granny's renewal. Is that what you're here about?"

"Yeah. So listen." He leaned forward. "Granny wants to do this on April twelfth. That's not exactly the day of the major standstill, but it's close enough. And she wants to go out when the moon is full."

I raised an eyebrow. "She's never struck me as someone with a flair for the theatrical."

"Oh, you'd be surprised." He sat back. "But that's not why she picked that day. The reason is sort of complicated, and it doesn't really affect what's going to happen, so we'll just leave it at that."

"Okay," I said slowly. "Is it her birthday?"

He rolled his eyes and looked away for a moment, then back at me. "You weren't supposed to guess," he said. "Yes, it's her birthday."

I smiled. "That's actually kind of poetic."

"It is, isn't it? That's our Granny for you. Anyway." He leaned forward again, forearms on his knees. "The thing is, we need to do this right at moonrise. Can you be there then?"

"Sure, no problem."

He reached behind him and extracted several sheets of paper, all stapled together, from a pile of debris on the floor. "Man, I've gotta clean this place up. Here." He handed the packet to me. It was a list of names and email addresses. "These are all of the people Granny has helped."

"All one-thousand-and-fifty-four?"

"Yeah. Granny wants you to invite 'em all to her renewal. She'd like to see everybody one more time before she crosses over." He tapped the papers. "Some of the email addresses probably don't work any more, but do the best you can."

"Okay. I'll email them all and tell them what time to be there."

"Great. That's perfect."

I folded the sheaf of papers in half and looked at him steadily. "Is there anything else I should be aware of? Any preparations I should make?"

He thought for a moment. "She didn't say anything about that. All she said was I should give you the list. I guess you'll know what to do when the time comes."

"That's how it's been working out so far," I said, and rose. "Thanks, Zed. I'll see you in April." I rose halfway, and then turned back. "Where *is* Granny, anyway? You never said."

He cupped one hand to his mouth and spoke in a stage whisper. "Don't tell her I told you this, but she's a little behind. She's finishing up the last couple of people right now."

"Oh." I glanced at the list. "Should I wait to send the invitations, then?"

He waved a hand. "No, no. Don't worry about that. Just send it. It'll be fine." He got up and opened the sliding door for me. "We'll see you in April."

"Sounds good." I stepped out and he followed me.

"Sure is nice weather today."

"We get these days sometimes in midwinter. They help keep us going until spring comes around again." I looked at him. "So what happens to you?"

"When Granny renews, you mean?"

"Yeah. You don't renew, too, do you?"

He laughed. "Nah, nothing like that." He leaned against the bus and stuck his thumbs in the front pockets of his jeans. "I don't know what will happen, to be honest. I guess we'll find out in April."

"I guess so. Well." I stood for an awkward moment, and then hugged him. "Thanks, Zed."

"Aw, Maggie." He hugged me briefly, and then stepped away. "You're her special one. She always says that. Except she still calls you Margie."

I laughed. "She's the only one who does. Rick doesn't dare."

"I'm glad that worked out for you." He smiled – a little sadly, I thought. It was only for a moment, though, and then he stepped back into the bus. "See ya in April!" he said, and with a final wave, he was gone.

As I walked up Eagle Mound, I replayed that scene in my mind. Had Zed been sweet on me all this time? It was possible. I could be pretty clueless about that sort of thing. I'd missed Rick's cues for years, after all. But I wasn't about to trade Rick for Zed – even if the deal did come with a VW bus that had been to Woodstock in '69.

Now here we were, on the day of Granny's renewal. I looked at the mound I stood on and saw in my mind's eye the way it had looked on the day I received my turtle, nearly two thousand years before. Then an odd thing happened: the memory from my vision overlaid reality. I saw both the grass-covered mound of today and the wooden screen that had been built to hide the preparation chamber behind.

Curious, I stepped to the edge of the partition and looked on the other side. There was my shaman – my partner in my past life. "This is a big moment," he said to me in the ancient language I only understood in visions. "Your first renewal ceremony. Do you remember what to do?"

"Of course," I replied.

He glanced toward the eastern hills. "It is time." He leaned forward swiftly and kissed my lips tenderly. "Keep the wheel turning for us."

I stepped back, and his image faded out. I could still feel his lips on mine.

I turned toward the east and saw my shaman had been right – the moon's disc was about to rise above the hills. I turned to the gathered crowd – the hundreds in this dimension who had come to say goodbye to Granny, and those who filled the circle in that long-ago time. "Listen!" I called, and they quieted. "Listen to me! We are about to partake in the sacred ceremony of renewal! Our purpose is to keep the wheel of time turning. The moon is at her peak tonight, but she has stalled in the sky. We must renew her with a sacrifice!"

A murmur went through the crowds. In the long-ago, a procession entered the circle through the opening opposite me; strong runners carried a catafalque upon which lay the body of a man. His hands lay upon his breast and his naked body had been prepared for this rite with herbs and oils. I grieved for him. He was the old shaman who had presented me my turtle.

In the current day, too, I grieved. For coming through the gate now was Zed, pushing a wheelchair that held a bent and wizened Granny.

I was shocked at her appearance. It had been years since I'd seen her; I'd talked to Zed a few times, but he always said she was busy saving her people. I wondered now whether she had simply been holed up somewhere, conserving her strength and waiting until this day.

The long-ago made its painfully slow way to the Eagle Mound; Zed took his time, too, wheeling Granny among those who'd come to see her off. I could see her nodding and smiling at each one, giving them a word, her hand, her blessing.

At last, the two processions reached the mound. "My dears," Granny whispered, "help me stand."

Zed took one of her arms and I took the other, and by main force we got her upright. As Zed wheeled the chair away, Granny took both of my hands in hers and said, simply, "This I give to you." And as my shaman partner had, she kissed me on the mouth.

A wind with the force of a tornado roared through me. "Kokumthena," I said, my senses reeling. For now I saw three images overlaid; the Hopewell crowd, anticipating their renewal; the crowd of today, anticipating Granny's; and the long, long view of a goddess, down all the years and centuries and millennia of time, when the wheel in the sky kept turning whether humans did anything about it or not.

I straightened – or the goddess did – and said, "Thank you, Lillian." Granny nodded, and seemed to fold in on herself. I caught her as the crowd in this time gasped. With Zed's help, I laid her out on the ground, exactly where my elderly shaman lay in a different time.

"We honor our warrior, who gave everything in the service to the spirits of this world!" I cried. "Be renewed, honored warrior, and may this ultimate sacrifice keep the wheel turning!" I raised my hands to the sky at the exact moment when the moon fully illuminated both bodies –

Granny's now and the shaman's in the misty past. Before my eyes – before all of our eyes – the bodies turned to smoke and wafted up, following the moonbeams to their source in the sky.

In the past, I said a few words of dismissal and the people slowly filed out of the circle.

In the present, chaos erupted under my shirt. I felt myself falling…

…I landed in a familiar place: the bank of the same creek where the Water Panther had attacked the confused doe. This time, though, the serpents were inside me, writhing and squirming until I felt like I was being torn apart. I screamed.

"You shall not!" That was the Thunderbird. I managed to look around; she sat in the tree near the river, shedding enough sparks to ignite the whole forest.

"Let her go!" That was Turtle. Concern and fear etched her features. Fear? Turtle was never afraid. What was going on?

Now a third figure joined them – a goddess with the mouthparts of a spider. "Kokumthena!" this newcomer roared. "You cannot do this! You must stop!"

"She is mine!" a muffled voice roared – mine, I realized, yet not mine. "I lay claim to her by blood! She is nothing to you!" The serpents inside me began roiling again, but I couldn't scream while Kokumthena had control of me. "Get…these…things…out of here!"

"And what was your claim on Lillian?" the Great Goddess cried. "She was not of your blood, but you seized her anyway."

"I took her *to get this one," Kokumthena said. "She's the one I wanted all along."*

Somehow, I found the strength of will to stand. "Well, you can't have me," I declared, and spat out a gust of wind. The serpents inside me settled immediately. The wind howled its fury, but could do nothing; at last, it blew itself out, leaving my ears ringing.

"Thank you," I said when I could speak again. "Thank you all."

Thunderbird settled her fiery feathers. "It was nothing. You have been ours longer."

"What she means," Turtle hastened to add, "is…"

"It's all right," I said. "I got the gist of it." I turned to the Great Goddess. "How long has she been pulling this?"

"Lillian was the first," she said. "When Spider Woman told me, I vowed she would be the last."

My eyes widened. "You set me up," I said. "That whole business about healing the rift between the Shawnee and the Nahua. It was all a ruse to get the water serpents inside me so they could be in position to kick Kokumthena out."

"It worked, too," she said gleefully. "I will take them back now, if you like."

"No," I said. "I rather like the notion that I can be both a creator and a destroyer." I looked at Turtle. "Do I still have to keep rescuing people? Setting them on their right path?"

Slowly, she smiled. "Does it matter? You would do that anyway."

"She should go back," Thunderbird said.

"I should," I said. "Thank you all again…"

I came to gradually. I realized I was lying on my back on the mound, in nearly the same spot where Granny had renewed.

"Maggie May!" Rick cried, and helped me up. He wrapped his arms around me. "Thank God. I thought…"

"It's all right, Rick," I said, pulling away to look in his eyes. "Truly."

"I could call 911," Randy said anxiously.

I looked around and realized everyone who had been at the ceremony was now crowded around us. I smiled and stepped away from Rick. "I'm fine, everyone, really. I just had something to settle with the gods. Please, go home. The ceremony is over. Thank you all for coming – I know it meant a lot to Granny."

I leaned against Rick and waved, smiling, until the crowd dispersed. "Thanks for coming," I called occasionally.

Randy wasn't fooled for a minute. "You're sure you're okay?"

"Do me a favor," I said. "When you get back home, go out to Canyon de Chelly and give Spider Woman my thanks."

"Sure," he said, eyeing me as if debating whether to say something. At last, he said, "Kokumthena wasn't supposed to possess Granny, was she?"

"No, she wasn't," said Zed, as he walked up the mound to join us. He looked older than I'd ever seen him, and very, very tired.

"The Great Goddess told me Kokumthena possessed Granny in order to get to me," I said. "Was that true?"

"Basically, yeah."

"And how long had she been dead?"

He looked at me in surprise. "Did you figure that out on your own, or did the Great Goddess tell you?"

"Does it matter?" I said. "How long?"

"The cancer did her in," he said. "About the time your mother's house burned down."

Mentally, I kicked myself. I knew at the time that something was off.

Rick looked shocked. "That was ten years ago."

"Yeah." Zed looked at the ground. "And I've been covering for her ever since. I'm not proud of what I did, but I didn't have any choice." He looked up. "Same as you, Maggie."

"No one's faulting you," I said gently. "So who are you really?"

He tilted his head and gave me a crooked smile. "Zedediah Jones. That part's always been true."

"And where do you go from here, Zedediah Jones?"

He sighed. "I have no idea."

"Come home with us, then," I said. "We've got room."

"Aw, Maggie, I couldn't," he said.

"Yes, you can," said Rick. "We insist."

His face split in a broad grin. "Well, okay! Thanks. And listen, don't think I'm some kind of charity case. I'll earn my keep. I can fix just about anything that breaks."

"Perfect," I said. "We could use a handyman. Come on." And I led the way out of the Great Circle and back toward the parking lot.

"I'll meet you there," Zed called, heading for his bus. "Thanks, you guys. This really means a lot to me."

We waved, and then turned to Randy, who had parked his rental car next to the RV. "Maybe I'll come live with you, too," he said, his eyes dancing.

"The door's always open," I said. "Seriously, come and see us."

"Maybe I will." He hugged me and shook hands with Rick, and got in his car.

The minute we were inside the RV, I tossed Rick the keys and settled into the passenger seat for the long ride to Rockville.

"So we're running a home for wayward souls now?" Rick said. "First Riley, and now Zed."

"Looks like it," I said with my eyes closed.

"Ruth would hate it, you know."

My lips curved into a wicked smile. "That's what I'm counting on."

Author's Note

I was happy to give Maggie a break in this book, after so much angst in the past couple of books.

Thanks as usual go to my editors extraordinaire, Susan Strayer and Kat Milyko, for their typical stellar job of keeping me from looking like an idiot.

So about this road trip. The route diverges a fair bit from Places Your Author Has Ever Been, so I had to seek answers a few times from the global zeitgeist. Thanks to the Facebook friends and friends of friends who helped me out with a couple of key issues: How dumb would it be to drive to Mexico City? And which L.A. neighborhoods should Abby, Sallie, and Emily live in?

Thanks, too, for those who helped by suggesting destinations for Maggie and Rick's road trip: among them, Kay Robinett, Hope Kadlec, and George Christ. That I asked for the suggestions as part of a contest had no bearing on their usefulness, or on my gratitude for the help.

If you enjoyed this book – or not – I'd love it if you would go back where you purchased it and post a review. Reviews are a key way that readers find good books, and I treasure each and every review that my books receive.

You're also warmly invited to join my Woo-Woo Team. We meet on Facebook at https://www.facebook.com/groups/WooWooTeam/. You have to ask to join, but so far I've let everybody in, so your odds of acceptance are spectacular. I'd love to see you there.

One more thing: To get the first word on all of my new releases, please click here to sign up for my spam-free newsletter. It's your guaranteed way to find out what's coming up, and I only darken your inbox with them three or four times a year.

Lynne Cantwell
Samhain 2017

About the Author

Lynne Cantwell writes mostly urban fantasy and paranormal romance, with a dash of magic realism when she's feeling more serious. She is also a contributing author for Indies Unlimited. In a previous life, she was a broadcast journalist who worked at Mutual/NBC Radio News, CNN, and a bunch of other places you have probably never heard of. She has a master's degree in fiction writing from Johns Hopkins University. Currently, she lives near Washington, D.C.

Discover other titles by Lynne Cantwell:

The Pipe Woman Chronicles Universe
Seized: Book One of the Pipe Woman Chronicles
Fissured: Book Two of the Pipe Woman Chronicles
Tapped: Book Three of the Pipe Woman Chronicles
Gravid: Book Four of the Pipe Woman Chronicles
Annealed: Book Five of the Pipe Woman Chronicles
The Pipe Woman Chronicles Omnibus

Where Were You When: A Land, Sea, Sky Anthology
Crosswind: Land, Sea, Sky Book 1
Undertow: Land, Sea, Sky Book 2
Scorched Earth: Land, Sea, Sky Book 3
The Land Sea Sky Trilogy

Dragon's Web: Book One of the Pipe Woman's Legacy
Firebird's Snare: Book Two of the Pipe Woman's Legacy
Spider's Lifeline: Book Three of the Pipe Woman's Legacy
Turtle's Weir: Book Four of the Pipe Woman's Legacy

A Billion Gods and Goddesses: The Mythology Behind *The Pipe Woman Chronicles*

The Transcendence Trilogy

Maggie in the Dark: Transcendence Book 1
Maggie on the Cusp: Transcendence Book 2
Maggie at Moonrise: Transcendence Book 3 (coming fall 2017)

Stand-Alone Novels

SwanSong
The Maidens' War
Seasons of the Fool

Short Story Collections

Back Home Again: The Five59 Stories, plus a few

Contributor

Indies Unlimited 2012 Flash Fiction Anthology
Indies Unlimited 2013 Flash Fiction Anthology
Indies Unlimited 2014 Flash Fiction Anthology
Indies Unlimited Tutorials and Tools for Prospering in a Digital World
Indies Unlimited Tutorials and Tools for Prospering in a Digital World,
Vol. II
13 Bites
Summer Dreams
Boo!: Volume 2
Winter Tales
Plan 559 from Outer Space
Other Realms
13 Bites Vol. III

I Heard It on the Radio
Plan 559 from Outer Space Mk. II
Other Realms Volume II
13 Bites Vol. IV
Plan 559 from Outer Space Mk. III
Free for All: A Writers' Anthology
13 Bites Vol. V

Find Lynne on Teh Intarwebz:

Facebook: http://www.facebook.com/pages/Lynne-Cantwell
Twitter: http://twitter.com/lynnecantwell
Google Plus: http://plus.google.com/+LynneCantwell
Goodreads:
http://www.goodreads.com/author/show/696603.Lynne_Cantwell
Blog: http://www.hearth-myth.com